Girl Made of Gold

Girl Made of Gold

Gitanjali Kolanad

JUGGERNAUT BOOKS
C-I-128, First Floor, Sangam Vihar, Near Holi Chowk,
New Delhi 110080, India

First published in hardback by Juggernaut Books 2020
Published in paperback by Juggernaut Books 2022

10 9 8 7 6 5 4 3 2 1

P-ISBN: 9789393986290
E-ISBN: 9789353451103

This is a work of fiction. Any resemblance to persons, living or dead, or to actual incidents is purely coincidental.

Typeset in Adobe Caslon Pro by R. Ajith Kumar, Noida

Printed at Thomson Press India Ltd

Girl Made of Gold

The Hunter

First he heard the crow. Crows know everything that goes on in their forest, and this crow, sitting on the branch of the jamun tree on the other side of the river behind the Shiva temple, had something important and curious to report. Again and again, he tilted his head this way and that to look down with first one yellow-rimmed eye and then the other, at something strange, then cawed his amazement and surprise. The tribal hunter, with his gourd for wild tomatoes and water chestnuts slung over one shoulder, armed with a catapult and throwing spear, squatted and watched the bird's unusual behaviour. Perhaps the leopard had killed a calf near the river and dragged it into the thick undergrowth there. Or could it be that a wild pig had fallen into a trap set by some other hunter? Now another crow came, and another, and they talked to each other in raucous, insistent tones. The hunter decided to go and investigate before darkness fell, or jackals would beat him to the prize. He marked in his mind the spot that troubled the crows and set off at a slow, steady run along the paths that only he and the wild animals used, which criss-crossed the townspeople's paths but remained hidden from them. Meat would taste good tonight.

As he neared the tree the crows cawed louder, telling the hunter he was now being mentioned in their conversation. But more than the sound told him he was near – he could smell freshly spilled blood. Then, with building disappointment, he knew what he'd find even before he saw it. He'd smelled that scent before, the distinct odour of his own kind, the thin-skinned ones, not much good for anything. In the thickest part of this jungle, between the back wall of the temple garden and the river, he saw the trail of disturbance, branches broken, the mat of fallen leaves churned up and the earth revealed where feet had kicked and dragged. There had been a struggle. Then in the puddle of blood, thickened but not yet completely dry, soaking into the soil and buzzing with flies, was the man's body, slumped against a tree trunk, jubba torn, dhoti open, komanam no longer covering his genitals. It was hidden only from the most superficial gaze, behind a thicket of bamboo.

The crows had already conducted their own investigation: he could see crow droppings on the man's dark curls, and the mark of the thick black beak in the wide open, staring eye. The hunter looked in the fast fading light for anything of value on the man's body. He ignored the gold ring and the diamond ear stud, for those could only lead to trouble. He saw a glint of silver grasped still in the man's hands, and took it from the dead fingers. It was a hair ornament, pointed and bloody at one end, and thickening to the width of his little finger at the other, with a parakeet's head, holding in its beak a piece of coral like the seed of a silk cotton tree. This he would wash clean of blood, and give to his woman, for she had long, thick hair. He would tell her nothing of the dead body. He would say he had found it on the bank of the river where the women bathed. He gathered up the few beedis that had fallen from a pocket of the shirt now gone, the box of matches, some two-rupee coins, a two anna and four pice.

He looked one last time at the body, and saw on the thigh where the pretty silver stick had gone in a small wound, but fatal, for the blood would have flowed from that place in spurts to the beat of his heart. The jackals were already waiting, would come as soon as it was dark, drawn by the scent of blood. They would start their feasting there, on the soft parts of the man. Then, being jackals, they would fight over the best meat, tearing his limbs, destroying his wholeness. The wild pigs, knowing themselves to be safe in the midst of such a feast, would root through his entrails, swallow his toes and his eyeballs whole, shitting out somewhere the gold and the diamond. Someone from the village might hear the noise of hyenas and wake from a dream or a nightmare that by morning would have been forgotten. Vultures might find some putrefying flesh dragged out into more open spaces. Maggots would grow fat on what was left, and crows and grackles would swoop down to eat the maggots. Ants and beetles would labour day and night carrying away even the flakes of dried blood, whatever hadn't soaked into the earth. Nothing would be able to grow there though, on the spot where the blood had pooled, not for a while. For many seasons, he would be able to make out the faint outline of that puddle.

The Priest

Before we enter the temple through the towered gateway, notice these unusual details. Usually the dvarapalakas guarding the entrance are ferocious male figures. But here, they are big-breasted females. Frightening nevertheless, one with her mace, the other with her curved sword. There is a reason for that. I will tell you the story when we are inside. First take a moment to look up and wonder at the gopuram, rising in seven diminishing storeys, capped by pot-like finials between the arched ends. Now you may step over the threshold. I will follow.

I understand your revulsion. It is only natural and I'm used to it. But if you want to get what you've come for, you have no other choice. I won't touch you.

Look there, ahead of us. We come to the Nandi, wearing a necklace of bells, with bells around his forelocks as well, his braided tail all decorated. This is a royal bull.

Let us begin the circumambulation. The shafts of the pillars along the corridor are called indrakanta, the eight sides polished to the smoothness of wood instead of being intricately carved. Notice the bases, with fish beings, mouths gaping, flaunting their flowering tails, and swans, with their necks entwined.

Stand here. Your gaze is drawn upwards to the frieze along the gallery. Have you ever seen its like? It is said that the sculptors were a father and son whose ongoing rivalry led to the special beauty of these carvings. Whatever the father carved on one side, the son matched on the other. The drummers seem to be nodding in time to the beat, and the flute players seem to be swaying to a lilting tune. The father carved this dancer here, so graceful you can almost hear her anklets jingle. Now look at the other side. The son, it is said, carved a dancer even more graceful, whose eyes seemed to dart from side to side. Late that night, the father came and carved closed the eyelids of the dancer. But what he did to spoil his son's work instead enhanced it. See? She seems to have closed her eyes in ecstasy.

The inscription reads, 'This shrine was caused to be made by the King of Immutable Resolve, as a receptacle for the elixir of precious gems that are his own good deeds.' Do you remember the story of King Manunitikanda? The king's young son, charging recklessly in his chariot through the streets of the town, drove his wheels over a calf, killing it. The grieving mother cow came to the court and rang the bell of justice. She demanded that the prince be killed in exactly the same way her own child had been killed. When none of his charioteers was willing to carry out this harsh punishment, the king himself whipped the horses on so that the great wheels crushed and mangled the young flesh, more precious to him than his own. Shiva is ever pleased by such displays of righteousness. Only the great god can weigh and judge. He restored both the calf and the prince to life. The raja who built this temple was a descendant of that heedless prince, who paid dearly for his carelessness, and then lived again, haunted by the memory of his own death. Do you ever think of what it must have been like to remember dying? I do, all the time.

The sacred tree of this temple is the jambu tree, sometimes called rose apple, or bull's heart. Do you want to taste the fruit? Go ahead. It is ripe. Does any comparison come to mind as you hold it in your hand? Look at this part here, where the flower has fallen off. Doesn't it look like lips, pouting to make the sound 'ooo'? Or you could say the fruit itself is shaped like a budding breast. But what does it matter, since every fruit and every plant and every flower suggests a woman. 'Her skin like a young mango leaf,' 'Her teeth like new buds on a palm tree.' So the poets say.

This temple came to be here because of this tree, and the suggestive nature of its fruit.

The raja, called Iravat, meaning rain clouds, was travelling with his retinue – servants, ministers, his favourite wife – along this riverbank.

I have calculated exactly when the events I am about to describe must have taken place. It could only have been on a Sunday, just as the rays of the sun lengthened before sunset. The king's beautiful consort, leaning out of her palanquin to admire the beauty of this scene, saw the ripe fruit hanging in abundance from the branches of the rose apple tree, and expressed her wish to taste it. The raja himself immediately alighted from his horse. While plucking the round, fleshy, pink-tinged fruit from the branches to satisfy the desire of his wife, desire arose in him. For is this not the very nature of desire? Desire awakening desire, never satisfied? So the sages warn us.

But kings do not heed the words of sages. The raja ordered his servants to set up camp right then and there so that he could immediately act on his amorous feelings.

Now it so happened that the royal astrologers had predicted that this raja would never have children. And for twelve long years, it had been so. I do not have his horoscope before me, but it is most likely that he had Taurus ascendant, given his dark skin, his regal status, his surrendering so readily to lust. Saturn, granting power, wealth and sexual prowess in the house he ruled, would exert his malefic influence on the house he aspected.

But on this occasion, the queen conceived. When it was clear that he was going to become a father, in refutation of all predictions, he immediately made a vow that he would construct a temple on the very spot of their union and finish it before the child was born.

Stonemasons laboured day and night cutting the stone, carving the pillars, making the gopuram. They chiselled the guardians of the entrance to represent the maids who had kept watch while the king and his consort sported in the grove. The frieze of celestial dancers and musicians look down from the heavens, providing divine accompaniment to the couples in the niches, in all the postures of lovemaking. The east-facing shrine they built to Shiva showing him in Vrishabhantika, as if standing and leaning on his bull. See? The bull is not there, but can be inferred from the position; so the raja himself with Taurus ascendant could imagine he supported the god. A shrine was built to Shanishwara, Saturn, his ruling planet, in a benign mood, with his two wives. The simplicity we now admire was a necessity, so that it could be finished within the time of the queen's confinement.

When the raja came with priests and musicians and dancers to complete the rituals by which the statues of the deities come to life with the god inside them, for some reason they were as if turned to stone, unable to move from this very spot. The time the astrologer had declared to be auspicious was about to pass.

One old priest understood the problem. He said, 'A shrine to Rahu must be constructed.' My surmise is that the raja had in his chart a Rahu yogakaraka, where this malevolent shadow ruled two houses in his natal chart. When he and his queen had congress under the jambu tree, it must have been Rahu kalam. Under ordinary circumstances, and for most people, such a time would not bring success to any venture. But for this king, with the particular positioning of Rahu in his chart, this was in fact the only time of the day when he could have succeeded in fathering a child.

The other priests began to argue about how to sculpt a deity in such a short time. Just then a monitor lizard was seen running across the spot and disappearing into a hole. That was a sign. The old priest said, 'This is where we must dig to make the shrine.' Right there under the earth was the deity, carrying sword and shield, cast in bronze, and shining like gold. That is the image you see. Thus, the raja's vow was fulfilled. The next day his wife gave birth to a beautiful baby boy. Our present raja is a descendant of the same illustrious lineage.

This temple was given into the charge of the old priest who understood the true nature of Rahu, a master of deception who hides behind fog and mist. The story of his origin gives a good idea of his character. When the gods set out to churn the ocean of milk for amrta, they needed the help of the anti-gods, the asuras. They said when the amrta rose to the surface, they'd share it. The asuras tried to take it all for themselves, but Vishnu as Mohini bewitched them and got it back, fully intending to give it only to the gods. But one asura didn't get muddle-headed by lust in Mohini's presence. He seated himself between Sun and Moon, and if they hadn't tattled on him, he would have succeeded in becoming fully immortal. As it was, he swallowed the nectar just in time, so that when Vishnu's chakra severed head from body both halves lived on. The shadow had become immortal along with the light. Rahu, the head with no body, can never be satisfied. And he hates Sun and Moon, getting his revenge by swallowing them whenever he can. Rahu is tricky, a blessing disguised as a curse.

Descendants of this priest, my ancestors, have been priests at this temple for I don't know how many generations. We are known for being able to handle the malevolent influence of Rahu. I will show you those inscriptions, written in an ancient script, confirming my rightful place within these walls.

My ability to see what others cannot has come to me as a gift. I didn't learn it, or develop it through practice. I have always been this way, for as long as I can remember.

But it has done me precious little good. I have not been able to prevent even one disaster in my own life, not one. We can't know ourselves, we stand in our own way, blocking the light that might illuminate our character. But perhaps what I see can help you. Maybe, maybe not. Not many who come here ever come back to tell if my spells and omens and incantations have worked. But whatever I see, I can't help seeing. I can tell many of your qualities by looking at your face. If you show me your palms, I can tell even more about your character. Disclose your name, and your date and time of birth, and you would be an open book to me. I will warn you of your fatal flaws. I do not look into the future, as many of my profession claim to do. I see patterns, that is all.

It is like this. If I write here in the sand a 3, then a 6 . . . you can only hazard a guess as to what the next number will be. It could be 9, it could be 12, almost any number is possible. But if I write 18 next, won't you feel certain that 108 must follow? So it is with human beings. The pattern of all that has gone before tells us what to expect next. This is what I believe. My ability is to see the pattern. What do I do? I just look, until the pattern reveals itself. Maybe anyone could do it, if only they stare long enough at what is right there in front of them. The world you see is not the world.

You have come all this way and I do not want to disappoint you. I think I know what you seek, but there is no simple answer to that question. I must tell the whole. There are many ways to tell a story. The storyteller may tell tales that go along like a river, smoothly or over rocks but continuously, always in one direction. That kind of story is called 'river's flow'. Or he may look back and then forward, as a lion looks, back towards his pride and forward towards his prey. Such a story is called 'lion's glance'. It is also possible for the story to jump from one event to another crossing great intervals of time and space. This manner of storytelling is called 'frog's hop'. Or a story may bring into close proximity different effects, different colours, different moods, like marigold, tuberose, margosa leaves in a garland. Such stories are called 'flower garland'.

Once when I was sitting on the riverbank, I saw a woman from the village wade out with her brass pot into the very deepest part of the river. There, barely balanced on the slippery rocks, with the current swirling all around, up to her hips, she put the pot in and filled it with the clearest, sweetest water. With the pot on her head, she fought her way back to the riverbank one step at a time.

Later on, when some pilgrim comes to the door of her little hut and says 'I'm thirsty,' she will pour the cool water in a steady stream into his cupped hands. He won't know how she stood there in the middle of the current and was nearly swept away, but his thirst will be satisfied. And I thought to myself, this is the storyteller's art. While immersed in life, while it swirls about and threatens to carry you away, you take a part of it and keep it with you. Later on, you pour it into the listener's ear. He won't know how you were in the events you describe, how you nearly drowned. He'll simply hear the story, he'll drink it in, it will satisfy his yearning.

The water has no beginning and no end, but the pouring does. Life has no beginning and no end, but the story must start somewhere. Listen.

Subbu

The statue appeared in the sanctum sanctorum. Just like that, like magic. In the days and weeks to come, when others told the story, they would start there, as if that was the beginning. Then they'd go backward and forward, picking up scattered pieces but never putting together the whole. Subbu hated to listen to them, and neither would he tell the story himself. He'd never even think of those events in the presence of others, in case the pain of remembering showed on his face.

There was a further problem. Even after all this time, he couldn't find the real beginning. When a koothu is about to start, the drummers play rhythms that build, telling the audience that any moment now the curtain will be pulled away. But there were no drums that day, no signal except a pain like a hammer pounding inside his head. He'd been restless, unable to sleep, impatient for the day to begin until it was almost dawn, when he'd been seized by the opposite impulse – to suspend time by keeping his eyes shut. But as the hour for the first puja neared and he heard the sounds of his uncle's early morning ablutions, he knew he couldn't put off his own rising and bathing any longer. Gripped by a dread that had no reason, he prepared himself for the day as if it was one like any other. The great god lying in the arms of his consort must be woken from his dreams at the proper time. This task must be performed, no matter what else troubled him.

The first puja to gently nudge the god out of slumber was conducted daily at five-thirty in the morning. Since only Subbu's inner churning intimated that this was not an ordinary day, he had no choice but to behave as usual and proceed with Uncle to the temple. Subbu's withered leg forced him to have an awkward, uneven limp, a condition he'd learned to manage, even matching Uncle's pace as he walked beside him. Uncle, however, never failed to mention the affliction and muttered as he always did, 'Poor boy. But what can we do? It is karma after all.' Subbu gritted his teeth and said nothing. Inside him, the suspense built up as if indeed there were drums reaching their climax.

They entered through the temple's outer gate. Subbu's skin prickled. Kanaka wasn't there. Finally, his unease matched with some circumstance in the outside world. Kanaka usually stood ready, bathed, her hair fragrant with jasmine, all the ritual objects arranged: the fresh milk, the flowers for offering just picked, the brass vessels gleaming. Instead, the plate and the pot were as they'd been left the night before, with nothing prepared for the puja. Uncle said, 'What can have kept her? She is never late.' They waited, Uncle impatient, Subbu aching with anxiety. Still, the puja must be conducted. 'Go and rouse her, that lazy girl, still wrapped in sleep.' Even in anger, he used no words of abuse like 'bitch' or 'whore', as he might have with the other dasi girls.

Subbu could tell from Uncle's voice that his scolding was only for show and hid an undercurrent of worry. He was more used to praising Kanaka for the skill and devotion with which she performed her ritual tasks. She'd never given Uncle any reason to complain about her services until this moment. Uncle well knew, as Subbu did, that she had not simply overslept. There must be some other explanation for her absence.

Subbu didn't protest; at least now he could take some action, however futile. Whatever had happened to Kanaka, the logical place to start looking for answers was where she had last been. If Kanaka's absence had an explanation it would come from her mother, Nagaveni.

The devadasi's house was not in the agraharam, but on the adjoining street separated only by the compound walls and the back lane that ran between. Though it lay equally close to the temple, Subbu would have to walk all the way around to approach it from the front, on the street in which those who were prosperous and of the upper castes but weren't Brahmins had their homes.

At any other time, Subbu would have welcomed an errand that took him into the domain of the devadasis. In the properly ordered world, with everything in its rightful place, the priests stride with justifiable pride. After all they know the Vedas, they keep the Earth on her course with their rituals, they have power over the fortunes of men. But the women in the Brahmin houses know nothing except how to make a proper rasam. They wear the nine-yard sari wrapped in such a way as to obscure the fact that they have breasts and two legs with hidden treasure between them. In the devadasi quarter it is altogether different. The women enhance the curve of their breasts with tight, short blouses and wear the sari tied low to show off their slender waists. They let their eyes wander up and down a man's body as if to say, 'You look like a tasty morsel!'

But this was not the moment to find pleasure in the beauty of women. Subbu called out as he entered the gate, 'Nagaveni amma, I'm here to fetch Kanaka.' A bright-eyed dasi girl unlatched the door and peeked out at him. He mounted the steps and stood on the threshold peering in, taking careful note of who was there and how they responded to the news of Kanaka's absence. The household had not yet fully awoken. He could see into the still shuttered back room, as Nagaveni, sleepy and fat, pushed herself into a sitting position with great effort. 'Kanaka? Kanaka? What do you mean? It is time for the ukshakala puja. She is at the temple of course. Where else would she be?'

'No. She is not there. That is why Uncle sent me . . .' Subbu's voice faded as he tried to interpret the look that came for a moment into those famous flashing eyes. Was she genuinely surprised to see him standing there? He couldn't be sure. Nagaveni, matriarch of the devadasi household, was an expert at dissembling.

'This makes no sense,' she said, looking around as if to spy Kanaka in some corner. Despite her great size, she rose gracefully to her feet, curves amplified into majestic presence. Her sari was in some disarray from sleep. When she raised her arms to her thick hair, still black and down to her waist, to twist and pull into a knot at her neck, Subbu's eyes went of their own volition to her bountiful breasts and lingered for a moment before he dropped his gaze.

The nadaswaram player Dorai came in from the back courtyard with a towel wrapped around his waist, working at his teeth with a neem twig. He looked Nagaveni over with the proprietary interest of a cowherd judging his prize cow, but her obvious worry wiped the smug satisfaction off his face. 'Didn't Kanaka come in last night, after making the garlands? We all saw her. Surely she left at the usual time this morning for her ritual bath. See, here is her bedding, rolled up just as it should be. There is no cause for concern.' He called upstairs to the nattuvanar, who was not one for rising early, it seemed. 'Ayya! Hey, Ayya!'

The man who wielded the cymbals so adroitly did not answer. Now this was unusual. The old man had been staying with Nagaveni while Kanaka prepared for her arangetram. His absence certainly required some explanation, and this seemed to be the first real clue. Could it be so simple? Kanaka had gone somewhere with her teacher, and all was well. Hearing Dorai continue to call, the harmonium player Nagarajan looked down from the landing and replied, 'Didn't Ayya tell you? He and Ganapathy had an engagement in Thirunelveli. The two of them left for the train station yesterday afternoon.'

'You were here all night, then. Any sign of Kanaka?'

'What do I know? Last night I lost at cards and drowned my sorrows. I was in no fit state to notice Kanaka's comings and goings.'

'Comings and goings? Comings and goings?' Nagaveni demanded. 'What are you suggesting?'

The wily musician, knowing well where his livelihood

lay, quickly made amends. 'Nothing, dear lady, nothing.' He came down the stairs, smiling his ingratiating smile, showing sharp white teeth and lips red with paan. 'Kanaka is like my own daughter, isn't she? I only meant that I myself, having played cards until late, having lost much money, and having drunk so much afterwards, would not have known anything even if a whole procession had come and gone.' Subbu could have sworn that his eyes were clear and wary. His statement contained at least two lies, but Subbu was in no position to confront him.

Ratnavalli, Kanaka's older sister, was nowhere to be seen. That wasn't surprising. She had her own fine house, coming only if Nagaveni specially called her, or there was a festival in which all the devadasis were involved. Vallabendran, her patron, was very generous and she was no doubt busy showing her gratitude for some trinket he'd given her, or using her wiles to wheedle one more out of him. Anyway, unless she could gain something, Ratna wouldn't even turn her face away from the mirror or slow the glide of her comb through her luxuriant black hair at the mention of Kanaka's absence. There was no love or closeness between the two sisters, but if Kanaka was in trouble, Ratna wouldn't have refused her help, surely. Could Kanaka be with her? These were questions Subbu needed to ask, but whom? And how? He had no standing to make inquiries like that.

Nagaveni questioned the other dasis and the servant girl, but no one knew anything about Kanaka's whereabouts. Then, taken with the sudden thought, Nagaveni said, 'Where's Durga? Durga's not here either. So she must be with Kanaka! Oh, what a relief! If the two of them are together, then there cannot be anything seriously wrong.'

Durga was Ratna's daughter by Vallabendran. Of course, no one would ever bother to question her, since she couldn't, or wouldn't, talk. Such a strange child, passive except for sudden bouts of trembling as if the air was filled with demons only she could see. Durga never looked at a person, or spoke, or played with other children, or accepted to be dressed or fed by anyone except Kanaka and Nagaveni. Ratna had given up on her when Durga was quite a small child, and it was Kanaka who'd cared for her like a little wounded animal. These days, if Durga wasn't sitting alone, quiet and with a vacant stare in a corner of the house, she could be found clutching and twisting a bit of Kanaka's dhavani in one hand, being led by it like a baby elephant twisting its trunk around its mother's tail. If anyone knew where Kanaka was, it would be Durga, even if she was not able to say.

All the worry seemed to drain from Nagaveni's face at the realization that Kanaka and Durga must be together, and she said, 'I'll come and do the puja today. I am the devadasi of this temple after all.'

Now they all followed Subbu back to the temple. The sun had not yet risen. A rooster crowed in the distance. Worshippers stood waiting in the still dark before dawn, clutching betel leaves and bananas. The lantern, swaying slightly in the breeze, threw distorted, moving shadows, giving the impression that the carved dvarapalakis, faces stern and forbidding, many arms brandishing weapons, were advancing and retreating, advancing and retreating. Uncle made a 'tchee, tchee' sound when he saw the crowd coming without Kanaka. He turned and led them to the main shrine, proceeding directly, without circumambulating, to the chamber filled with darkness, the garbhagriha. They all followed him because at that moment it seemed as if it was the puja that was most important, that Kanaka's non-appearance had some simple explanation; she would come running now, any minute, and take her place. Subbu wanted to shout, 'Let's not waste time! We must look for Kanaka, before it is too late.' Why was he so troubled by an absence that seemed to bother no one else? He had no answer to his own question, so he kept his mouth shut, and held the lantern up so that everyone could see their way through the dark passage.

When they reached the sanctum, Subbu put down the lantern and unlatched and pushed open the two sides of the door. As he folded the second side back to fully reveal the lingam supported and contained by the yoni, the emblem of the great god, something behind the door clattered, but no one else seemed to notice, so Subbu said nothing. Uncle recited the proper Sanskrit verses, then tried and failed, tried and failed to light a match and put it to the wick of the large brass lamp in front of the lingam. Finally Nagaveni came forward, took the matchbox from his hand and struck the match so it flared. She cupped it and lit the four wicks one after the other. A devotee reached up and struck the bell. Uncle then bent and held the camphor to the lamp's flame for the arati with the pot lamp, the devadasi's ritual task. Nagaveni accepted it from him and stood ready, in front of the lingam. As she began the circle, the burning camphor illuminated a little statue at the god's base. Nagaveni cut short the upward curve of her movement and stood transfixed. The circle of devotees gasped. Reflecting the flickering flame, it shone like gold against the black mass of the great god. Just as the camphor finished burning, the lamp also went out. Later, as the story was told and retold, it became a breeze like a sigh, a soft breath scented with clove, that blew out the flame, leaving the sanctum filled once more with darkness.

As the lamp was relit, the air was alive with the sense of unified expectancy, all eyes fixed on the little golden statue standing on the pedestal of the lingam. Nagaveni cried out.

Dorai leaned in to get a better look and the harmonium player threw up his hands in a theatrical gesture of wonder. Uncle whispered, 'Shambo, Shambo,' and the other devotees repeated, 'Shambo, Shambo.' 'Shambo' echoed in the dark chamber of the sanctum sanctorum where the one lamp flickered. The statue, a hand's height, was of a slim girl, small, round breasts and slender waist, standing with a graceful bend at the hip, feet together, hands in pushpanjali as if offering jasmine flowers. Kanaka was not where she should be, and instead this statue had appeared. Someone said 'Kanaka' and Nagaveni repeated it, 'Kanaka!' Subbu could not be sure if her response was genuine sudden insight or misdirection, subterfuge.

'It *is* the very image of Kanaka,' the priest said. He was the only one who had the right to enter the sanctum so he lifted the statue and brought it out, examining it carefully. Everyone crowded around to get a better look. The statue seen up close was very fine, with each detail – eyebrows, eyelids, nostrils, full lips and small chin – delicately modelled. It was a lamp, meant to hold oil and wick in cupped hands. 'She will continue to dispel the darkness just as Kanaka did when she performed the arati.' 'Look how her plait is made, with four strands instead of three.' Nagaveni, so proud of Kanaka's thick hair, had been in the habit of dividing the hair into four parts to make the special braid called 'belt braid' for the way it hung so straight and flat. This kind of braid was more difficult and time-consuming to make, but Nagaveni insisted on it for Kanaka. The golden statue's braid was just the same.

No one knew, or admitted to knowing, how the statue came to be in the sanctum sanctorum; everyone considered it to be a miracle, a statue of Kanaka appearing in place of the real girl. Even Nagaveni seemed to accept that nothing further needed to be done and that the appearance of the statue was all the explanation that Kanaka's disappearance required. If she had any reservations about the miracle, she was keeping them to herself.

Subbu wanted to shout, 'No, it is nothing more than a statue. We must go and look for Kanaka. We must find her,' but he said not a word.

Nagaveni had performed the ritual service at the temple until Kanaka took over. So now she accompanied Uncle to complete the ritual worship of the gods and goddesses in the other shrines. Those who had been present at the puja left quickly, eager to gossip about what they had witnessed.

Subbu returned to the sanctum to check what had fallen when he'd pushed open the door. It was a brass lamp, a small one, usually kept in the niche at the main entranceway. Subbu could think of no reason it should have been placed behind the door to the sanctum. It told him nothing except that someone, a human being who needed light, had been in there between the time of the last puja the previous evening and this morning's first puja. Had this person placed the statue where it had just been found? Why? And who would dare to enter the sanctum? Uncle, of course, but he seemed incapable of such pretence. Another Brahmin priest? But this small temple only employed the one, Uncle. Would anyone else risk the wrath of the deity to enter that sacred space? He held the small ordinary brass lamp in his hand, looking down at his feet to where the oil had spilled when the opening door had knocked it over, and picked out of the pool of oil the wick, burned almost to the end. In fact, it may have been still burning and been put out only when it fell over. Carrying the lamp with him to return it to its proper place, he bowed out of the sanctum and pulled shut the door and latched it.

As he turned, he glimpsed small feet showing from behind a pillar. It was Durga, sitting as she often did, staring without expression at a point on the floor in front of her. Where had she come from so suddenly? Had she been there all along and no one had seen her? She gave no indication that she noticed his presence. It wasn't that Durga was mute, for, once in a while, without any training, and only when she chose to, she sang fragments of the songs she heard her mother and grandmother sing. No one had ever managed to get her to talk, but she had the capacity. She could, Subbu thought, be made to talk, somehow. He shook her hard, and she dropped what she'd been clutching tight in her fist. He picked it up. It was a thin strip of cloth, torn from a dhavani. He said fiercely, 'Tell me where Kanaka is! Tell me!' But she seemed not to feel Subbu's grip on her shoulder, so finally he gave up and left her sitting as still as if she was carved in stone. Nagaveni would have to find a way to deal with her now that Kanaka was gone.

When the ritual worship at all the shrines was completed and Nagaveni had taken the brass vessels and lamps for cleaning, Subbu and the old priest returned to their house in the Brahmin quarter. Subbu finally spoke up.

'How can a girl turn into a statue? We should search for Kanaka. If you accept something that can never happen, others will do nothing.'

'Chee! It is a great day for our temple. Keep your mouth shut. As if you know everything.'

'Flesh can't turn into metal, Uncle. Kanaka could be hurt or sick or lost somewhere.'

'Somewhere? Where would Kanaka go? This village is not so big. Let me tell you, such miracles have happened many times. Ahalya turned into a rock and back into a woman again at Rama's touch.'

'In stories, Uncle. This is real life.'

'It is true. Such things were more common in the past. In the Kali Yuga we are not destined to witness such miracles often. But in my own lifetime, this is not the first time such a thing has happened. There was Ramalinga Swami, from my district. Such a holy man, who saw god as pure light. In front of all his disciples, he entered his room, a small room, with no other means of going in or out, saying, "I will not be visible to your eyes for a certain period." The disciples lay down and slept right there in front of the door. The next day, he didn't come out, nor the next day, nor the next. Finally the disciples, fearing that he was ill or hurt, broke open the door. There was no one there, nothing, except in the darkness a light like a thousand glow-worms. This happened near our native place, in Vadalur, when I was eight years old and your mother was yet to be born. Even the British collector and the tahsildar came to investigate his disappearance. The event sparked a wave of devotion across the countryside. Everywhere they sang his songs, "The lord who is the dancer, dances in the public hall / And he doesn't know his caste or his country". This is just like that.'

'It's not. Kanaka was no saint; she was just an ordinary girl. You yourself called her a goose only yesterday, at the puja in the evening, when she was so slow to do her steps, and stood there daydreaming.'

'That was my mistake. Now I recognize her greatness.'

'If the statue is supposed to be Kanaka, our Kanaka, then how does it come to have such huge jimikis hanging from her ears, the like of which Kanaka never wore? Did she pray, "Dear god, I can't bear this life, turn me into a statue, and also give me some jimikis"?'

'Now you tell me something, since you have all the answers. How did the statue get there, then, into the sanctum? You and I are the only two allowed to enter the womb house. No one else would dare risk polluting the great god by such an act. Poor girl! She had no choice but to beg the god for mercy. Even in the dancing girl caste I can't believe such things go on. Through this miracle Kanaka has been saved from a fate worse than death.'

Subbu's mother, Brhadambal – who had been preparing the idlis for breakfast in the kitchen while listening to their argument – came with the brass plates and placed them on the floor. The story of the golden statue had reached her ears even before her son and brother had returned home. Now she chimed in, 'Everyone is so quick to condemn Vallabendran, as if he is not a noble man. We shouldn't talk like that. We live under his patronage, and we have often experienced his generous nature. First of all, who knows whether he actually sent the tamboolam for Kanaka. I say if he hasn't done so, maybe he never will. So why start condemning him. And even if he did make an offer for Kanaka's first night, would he ever have made such a move unless he knew something outside of common knowledge? After all, he is the one best positioned to know of the intimate relations within the devadasi household.'

Uncle sat down in front of his plate, saying, 'But the girl called him "Appa", so how would she feel? Innocent as she was, she had the power of her chastity. When she appealed to the god, he protected her.'

'Kanaka is a devadasi. How can she have the power that comes from chastity? I say, no, only the faithful wife has karpu like that. Anyway, what need of god with Nagaveni for a mother. As if she would have allowed such a thing to go on if Kanaka was really Vallabendran's child! She has her own way of handling things. Maybe this is her doing. Just like Nagaveni to get Kanaka out of Vallabendran's way with a ruse that enhances her own standing in the world. I don't put any act of cunning beyond Nagaveni. I wouldn't be surprised if Ratna goes to visit a relative and Nagaveni embarks on a pilgrimage, and all three have disappeared. Next we'll come to hear of two sisters dancing on the stage in Madras before dignitaries, just like the Kalyani Sisters or the Jeyaratnam Sisters. The names will be different but it will be them. Nagaveni may look very high for a patron for Kanaka and she knows it. Now, Subbu, come and eat the idlis before they get cold.'

Uncle retorted, 'And where did Nagaveni get a gold statue

in Kanaka's image? Such a beautiful and precious thing is not so easily obtained. You haven't seen it yet. Its beauty proclaims its divinity.'

Subbu protested, 'How can we argue like this over a statue? I can't just sit here and eat when Kanaka is missing. The statue is not Kanaka! Everyone has gone mad to say it looks like her. It looks nothing like her. We need to search for her right now!'

'Search for her? You may search for her, but you won't find her. She's gone where no human being can follow. I must ask Vallabendran for the funds to build a shrine for the statue. I'm sure that as the news of this miracle spreads, pilgrims will come from far and wide to worship here and invoke her blessings. Our deity will take the name "He With the Golden Attendant". I must add her story to the stalapurana of the temple.'

Uncle was impervious to every argument, and Subbu's mother was no help at all. Though she'd earlier expressed her own cynical view that the statue's appearance in the temple was no miracle but somehow Nagaveni's doing, faced with her brother's judgement on the subject, she deferred to him. Resolutely orthodox, she believed whatever the male of the household said on any matter not to do with the kitchen was not to be questioned. She could see how much pain inaction was causing Subbu, but she wouldn't go against the prevailing wisdom expounded by her elder brother. Now she harangued Subbu in a soft but insistent tone. Subbu shook his head in despair, wishing as he had so many times before that his father hadn't gone off and abandoned him to people who couldn't be bothered to think.

It had been more than eight years since his father had left, half Subbu's lifetime, but he was still spoken of and remembered as a wise man whose judgement could always be trusted, one who never said a word he hadn't considered deeply. Would he ever have accepted the story of Kanaka's death and miraculous transformation? Subbu said to his mother, 'Shut up! Father might never have left if you didn't talk so much. He couldn't stand the sound of your endless yakking.'

'Me? I'm the one who can't open my mouth in this household, who cannot even call you for your meals without some complaint.'

'If only you'd been a different kind of woman, he would have stayed, and I'd have had a father.'

'What do you know. If I'd been a different kind of woman your father would not have married me. He needed someone to take care of his old parents, didn't he? I knew the right way to run a Brahmin household. My dowry was needed to arrange the marriage of his younger sister, your aunt in Madurai. My jewels paid for that wedding. Now look where she is in life and where I am. I came into this household with one diamond nose ring, a pair of ruby earrings and six gold bangles on each hand. The diamond's gone, replaced by glass, the rubies too, and just one thin wire around each wrist. He took what he needed and then he left. He's not here, so you miss him, but what about me? I'm around every day, doing everything for you, only for you. If not, why wouldn't I just go to the Ganga and die there? I should achieve moksha too. I'm your mother. If I'd been another kind of woman, my son would have been very different from you.'

Subbu had heard this speech many times. 'Shut up, please, just shut up! Can't you see that no man can stand your endless nagging? Why didn't you say no to him when he asked for your bangles? Instead you gave them to him, just so you could remind him every day of your sacrifices.'

'You know nothing of my sacrifices! If there were six pieces of drumstick in the sambhar, didn't I serve you three first, and then two more when you said, "Amma, this is very good"? Only one piece for Uncle, and none for me. Don't be so greedy, then I won't have to sacrifice, day after day.'

'Has there ever been a day when you haven't had the last word? You are right, you are perfect, I wonder if you'll find even heaven good enough for you.'

'Go on, curse me, wish me dead. I have you to light my funeral pyre, so why would I complain.'

The rosewood desk with the blue glass ink bottle and the pen sitting ready for work, with his notebooks and the books he'd used for his astrological calculations in the drawers beneath, were the tangible reminders that Subbu had of his father. One morning Subbu had opened his eyes to the full light of day, wondering why he'd been left to sleep as long as he wanted instead of being forced to get up at dawn. He'd gone into the kitchen rubbing the sleep from his eyes, to find for the first time in his life that the fire had not been lit and food was not being prepared. His mother hadn't even bathed. She was sitting with her head on her knees, and when he touched her shoulder, she turned her face to him with eyes reddened from crying. She said in a flat voice, 'Your father is gone.'

'Gone? Gone where?'

'Gone, just gone. Who knows where men go when they abandon their families.'

'Who will do the pujas in the temple?'

'Your uncle, my older brother, is coming to take his place. He has made all the arrangements.'

'Did you say anything to try and stop him? For my sake at least? Did you? Did you?'

'He's your father, Subbu. Have you ever known him to listen to me?'

'You're happy that he's gone, aren't you? Now you can do

everything your way. You can do exactly as you like. But I won't obey you. I'll do what I like too and you can't stop me.'

Subbu had never heard fights between his mother and father. That was not their way. Instead, they'd used a rich vocabulary of silences. When his mother asked a question, his father would let the long pause before he answered convey his displeasure. And his mother would never answer back, but would shout at the servant girl or go into the kitchen and begin pulverizing something with the grinding stone. In time to the rumble of granite against granite, she would carry on a conversation with herself or the world at large, telling her whole life story to justify whatever she had done that had angered him. 'I was born in an agraharam, and believe it or not, as you please, I have grown up in that way, doing things as they ought to be done. My mother trained me; she herself was a priest's wife. From a young age I helped her in every task. Did I play childish games? Ask anyone in my village, they'll tell you, no one ever saw me play in the dirt. Instead, I learned how to pound the rice, grind the spices, store the grain, how to prepare each and every vegetable in season. So why should Subbu's father say, "What is the need for such rich food every day?" when all I asked was which vegetable he preferred? "What you like," but at the same time, "not rich"! What am I to make of such an answer? Do I ask for money for extra ghee? Never. With whatever I am given to manage the household, I manage. I have no problem. The world might be a cruel place but here you should feel satisfied, that is my aim. Gods must be fed and dogs must be fed. That is what my mother always used to say.'

Subbu understood his father's need to get away from that relentless voice. He limped out of the house as Brhadambal called after him, 'Where will you look? Eat a little before you go, can't you?' Subbu set off towards the devadasi quarter once more. He would talk to Nagaveni. Maybe he could trick her into telling him something. If that didn't work, he would get hold of Durga. She'd been in the temple after all, and Kanaka was the only one who could have taken her there. The little girl, spending all her time with Kanaka as she did, must know everything. If only he could get something sensible out of her.

As he made his way along the street, leaving the Brahmin houses behind, he realized that the two boys strolling in front of him were discussing the statue in the temple and Kanaka, and not with any reverence. When he understood what they were saying, Subbu couldn't control himself. He shouted, 'You dirty lying prick, you dog, you son of a whore. You never touched her.'

'Oh, I touched her all right. She had had enough of you, Cripple. She wanted a real man so she came to me.'

'Shut up. Shut your ugly mouth!'

'Or what, Cripple? What will you do to me? I licked her hairy slit and she liked it. Now everyone talks as if she's a saint, but we all know she's a whore. And you, Crippled Brahmin Boy, weren't you her pimp?'

Subbu caught up with the boys as they stood there taunting him. He swung his fist as hard as he could at the boy's head, but he had no experience of fighting. The boy dodged easily, and Subbu lost his balance and fell. He struggled to get back up, but with nothing to hold on to, he could get no further than on to his hands and knees. The boy came closer and pushed him back down, holding him there with his foot on his neck, laughing and ridiculing him. 'Brahmin curses bring us good luck, didn't you know? Curse all you like.'

The goldsmith's wife came out of her hut and chased the boys away. She helped Subbu to get up. 'You're going to be crippled for the rest of your life, Subbu.' She brushed the dust off his bare chest and shoulders. 'You need to let those words roll off you, like water off a lotus leaf. As if Kanaka would have been bothered. She'd know exactly how to answer boys like that. She'd say, "Boasting, as if it's a sugarcane stalk, when all the girls complain it's a toothpick." Now that she's not here to protect you, you better learn to take care of yourself.'

Subbu mumbled his thanks, turning his face away so

she couldn't see how his lip trembled. He squeezed his eyes tightly shut to keep from crying. Without Kanaka, the world was a harsh, unfriendly place with no one in it he truly cared about.

He couldn't continue to Nagaveni's house now that he'd been polluted by the touch of those ruffians. He'd have to return home to bathe and change his clothes. He needed to solve the mystery of Kanaka's disappearance, which seemed to be connected to the statue's appearance, so that mystery too required his consideration. After that, maybe he, too, like his father, would go to some place where no one knew him.

After his bath, he went up to the terrace. It was hot there, but one corner, which fell under the shade of the neem tree, was a safe refuge where he wouldn't be disturbed.

Kanaka had been part of his life from the moment Nagaveni brought her home after her confinement. Since he'd been only a baby himself, he had no memory of a life without her in it. When they were growing up his feelings for Kanaka were simply an aspect of his life, hardly noticed. Just like a limb, used without conscious thought until it was hurt – only when those feelings caused pain did they come to his awareness. They'd been children then, ten years old, playing in the temple garden early in the morning, after the first puja finished. She had to gather flowers for the rituals: oleander, marigold, jasmine. He was helping her only because the sooner she finished her work, the sooner they could start their games. An indifferent sun, a grey sky with grey clouds, the roosters crowing. They reached on tiptoes for the jasmine flowers. She said, 'Let's see who's taller,' and turned and pressed herself against him, her back to his. She was tall for her age. He could feel the wings of her shoulder blades against his, her hair like a silk rope along his spine, as she reached up her hand to rest on both their heads. He was struck dumb by the sudden surge of blood in his loins.

'You're taller,' she said, 'by this much,' showing him the width of two fingers. 'But I'm still faster,' and she'd taken off, her skirt belling behind her and revealing her round calves narrowing into her heels, the pale soles of her feet flashing in the dust.

In the same instant he knew his feelings for her, he knew they must be hidden.

He ran after her as fast as he could. Her long braid thrashed and coiled like an angry snake. He reached out and caught it, pulled hard, held her back, passed her. He reached the tree first and fell panting and breathless at its base. She wasn't running any more.

'Cheater.'

'Whore.'

'Eunuch.'

'Bitch.'

'Cocksucker.'

She went back to plucking flowers with the air of a grown-up who had serious work to do. The outline of the small buds of her breasts through the thin cloth, a sight that had never affected him before, now made him sick. He couldn't bear to look or turn away. He was frozen by the knowledge that had come to him. In that moment he knew what it signified, exactly as a sound connects with its meaning. This realization had tipped him from one world into another, in which everything looked the same, but now a tree was more than a tree, and every leaf that fluttered at the ends of its branches had its own secret.

Nonchalant, she was humming one of her songs. He kicked dirt at her as he walked past, and muttered, 'Slut.' She kept on humming as if she hadn't heard, ignoring him in a most irritating way.

So what? He had other things to do. As soon as he was out of her sight, he ran home. He tried to sneak in into the house, but his mother heard him. She said, 'Come, Subbu darling, coffee is ready. Wash up now. Have you seen Uncle? Call him too.'

He shouted, 'Shut up. Shut up. Stop bothering me with your nonsense.' He unrolled his mat and threw himself on it, pressing his cheek to the cool cement floor. His mother fussed around him, wanting to feel his forehead, but he wouldn't let her. He lay there clutching his stomach as if in great pain. He rolled around on the ground and moaned; he pressed the heels of his hands against his eyes.

He'd always eaten before he was hungry, fallen asleep before he could fully know his tiredness. That had changed. He'd had a taste of desire.

What he wanted, if he could express it, was to have no one anywhere around when he and Kanaka stood together in each other's presence. In a forest, or in a room in a palace somewhere, with no one else in the whole kingdom. He thought to himself, 'I'd give anything.'

And later, was it a week or a month, the two events so connected in his mind that there seemed to be no exact time between them, the fever had come in earnest. He'd been sick for a long time, and she had come and sat by him, she'd held his hand, she'd told him stories, she'd sung to him. 'She cared for you like a sister,' his mother said. 'She kept you cool. If it wasn't for Kanaka, it might have been worse.' When the illness had finally abated, he was left with the withered left calf and foot. Kanaka sat with him and talked while the other children played games he couldn't join. She ignored his anger and bitterness, teased him as she always had. He'd leaned on her to learn to walk again, with that ugly limp. And in the years after, she'd slowed her own pace to match his. He'd hated himself for crying in front of her over the pain and the sad loss and the way his life would now be forever blighted by his condition. She had consoled him, 'What does it matter? It is not the best thing, but it is not the worst either. I will always be near you to help you.' He would never measure himself in relation to her again. And he'd got exactly what he'd wished for. He'd given everything, and he'd got to be with her, alone with her, but not in a way that satisfied his yearning.

He was aware of those qualities that others praised, her golden skin – Kanaka Kanaka Kanaka – her hair down to her hips, her lotus petal eyes. He told himself, 'She has two of them, just like everyone else,' except the blind beggar at the temple entrance, who made a virtue of necessity, as he himself must learn to do. But he didn't love Kanaka for that. He loved that golden skin because it was her skin, the dimpled smile that showed small, sharp teeth between full lips because it was her smile. And now she was gone.

When he'd seen her the evening before, she'd spoken words that had made him uneasy even as he'd heard them, without knowing why. Now that she'd vanished, he needed to recall that conversation exactly and try to interpret her words in the light of what had happened next – the statue, her disappearance.

Yesterday she'd come to find him, actually sought him out in his favourite spot where in the old days they'd played together, under the banyan tree near the boundary stones of the village. It had been a long time since she'd made any such effort. He'd thought at first it was a return to that old relationship, when they'd been friends. He'd been so happy seeing her approach as the late afternoon sun threw long shadows. He'd stopped practising tricks with his top and tried to hide it behind his back because last time she'd been dismissive of his skills, deeming them childish. But now she said, 'No, don't stop. That's a clever trick. Do show me again.' He set the top spinning with one swift throw and jerk of the string, then looped the string around to pick it up, still spinning. 'Put out your hand, straight out.' She'd done so, and he'd released the top on her palm. She'd said, 'Look, it moves and bounces as if it's alive. It tickles.' For one moment, he'd thought, 'Kanaka has returned to me,' as the purest joy poured into him.

But as their conversation continued, it seeped slowly out again. She seemed determined to be as she used to be, but it required an effort of will. Her voice was brittle and tight, her laugh expressed no mirth.

'Listen, Subbu. I've been very distant, I suppose you've noticed.' She didn't look at him directly as she spoke, but just past him, over his shoulder.

'Yes, you got tired of me. I don't blame you. I'm tiresome, I know. You must have been sick of my complaining.'

'You were never the reason. Whatever it was, it wasn't an excuse to treat a friend the way I treated you. I've been feeling so bad about it.'

'Don't say any more, Kanaka. I don't need any apology from you.' He'd clasped his two hands tight to stop them from trembling.

She'd come and put her hand on his shoulder and looked into his eyes for a moment before looking away again. 'No, I have to say what I've come to say.' And he'd felt almost desperate to stop her, knowing that whatever came out of her mouth next would destroy his peace. 'Why talk of bad things? You've said enough.'

'Subbu, don't turn away, let me say it. It's better if I do it now, I don't know when I'll have another chance. Come, sit down beside me.' She helped him sit down on the thick twisted roots of the banyan tree.

'I've lied to you, and said harsh things I didn't mean.'

'It doesn't matter, the past is past.'

'These past few months, we've fought so often. I want you to know in every case you were right and I was wrong. I called you stupid and blind and an idiot, only because I didn't want to admit my mistakes. You thought there was something wrong with you, and really it was something wrong with me. Do you forgive me for that?'

'Why are you making so much out of nothing? I don't even remember. Who cares.'

But he did remember. And it was true, he'd thought, more than once, he was going mad.

'It matters because . . . you are my oldest friend. There is one day in particular that I can't forget. Remember when I dropped the washed brass vessels?'

He could recall the day she spoke of with particular vividness. In the temple, she'd suddenly turned as he was in the middle of his awkward lopsided step, and the bad leg, over which he had so little control, had come in her way and she'd stumbled, dropping all the vessels she'd been carrying. He'd started to apologize but before he could get out a word, Kanaka had shouted angrily, 'You clumsy oaf. Now look what you've done. You're supposed to help me but you're no help to anyone. Go away with your ugly leg and let me get my work done in peace.' This was so uncharacteristically cruel of Kanaka that Subbu had looked at her in shock, the tears coming unbidden to his eyes. 'Don't start crying like a baby the way you usually do. I've got to do this washing all over again, and I don't want you around to slow me down.'

The pain of Kanaka's words had burned inside him for days. She'd never before referred to his crippled leg like that. It was not that she didn't get irritated with him. Always in the past, though, her natural sweet temper modulated her sharp remarks. If she said 'Can't you stop yakking and let me have a few quiet moments?' he'd go off and pointedly sulk until she relented, saying, 'I didn't know my own thoughts could be so boring. I'm sorry I scolded you. Tell me something interesting you read in a book,' and the small rift that had opened in the space between them would quickly close, the scolding itself a sign of their intimate and unbreakable connection. But this incident with the vessels had marked the end of their easy camaraderie. She had not tried to smooth things over. From then on she'd avoided him and he hadn't found the words he wanted with all his heart to say. She was suddenly too grown up for guessing games, or even five stones, which had been her favourite. She'd stopped telling him long stories of all that went on in the devadasi household, of Nagaveni and Ratna and the great Vallabendran on whom they all depended. Though they'd been playmates all their lives, she had turned just like that into a stranger, leaving him without a friend. For a while he'd continued to chase after her, but whenever he did manage to catch up with her somewhere, she'd been quick to make excuses and rush off. Finally he'd given up trying to talk to her or play with her, but though she'd left him behind, he never left her, not in his heart. He'd watch her from a distance, or stand where he knew she'd pass, so they'd have to meet, even if only for a few minutes of formal conversation that made him feel sick at the end of it, as if they were nothing to each other.

Subbu didn't want to dwell on that past now. He tried his best to stop her talking in this serious way.

'But that was my own clumsiness! You had all the work of washing everything again, going to the well, drawing the water. I don't blame you. I cursed myself.'

'You didn't trip me, I did it on purpose.'

That took him by surprise.

'Did what?'

'Dropped all the vessels.'

'But why?'

She studied him, then shook her head, not saying what she'd been about to say.

But why was Kanaka telling him all this? He said, 'Let's talk about something else.'

'No, one last thing. Here, you must take this back.'

She held out her left wrist to him. On it was a black string with fourteen knots, an amulet he'd tied and said mantras over to safeguard her from the evil eye.

'Why? It won't do you any harm, Kanaka. It will only protect you.'

'What protection, Subbu? If I protect myself from fire with water, and end up drowning, what good is that? I want . . . whatever is coming to me . . . to come. Take it off my wrist and throw it into the river.'

'Please keep it, for my sake.'

'No, it must come off, and you must remove it, since you tied it.'

'Are you sure?' She nodded. Subbu undid the knot with unsteady fingers, and tucked the string into the waist of his veshti.

'We are a pair, aren't we, Subbu, you with that leg, and me with . . .' There was a long pause as she slipped into a reverie.

'There is nothing ugly about you, Kanaka. You're a . . .' What was the most perfect thing to which he could compare her? A flower? A fruit? The moon? 'A lotus,' he finally said. 'There is not one thing about you that is not perfect.'

'Look again, my friend. Look closely.' And she'd turned back to face him. He'd stared at her for a long time, searching for the imperfection she wanted him to see but not finding it. Her eyebrows were curved like swords, her eyes were like spears, red-tipped from piercing hearts, just as the poets sang. He inhaled the smell of jasmine flowers in her hair, and of the sandalwood that overlaid and mingled with her own smell. He wanted desperately to touch her, find with his fingertips the place on her cheek where the dimple appeared when she smiled, press his lips to the curve of her neck, but he knew that would spoil everything.

'No? You don't see it? It's staring you in the face.'

'I see only Kanaka, only gold.'

'Oh Subbu. You and I, we've been together so long. Look

at me now as if you didn't know me at all, as if you don't even know my name.'

What did she want him to see? He closed his eyes, then opened them to look intently at her again, and she let him look. He tried to forget the words of the poets he'd seen her through and observe only what was there in front of him. While he looked at her, the deep centre of her eye looked back into him, reflecting everything that was in his heart. For a moment, laid bare to her, he felt it, her strangeness. They were floating somewhere out in space. But in the very next instant, he knew where he was, and the face became Kanaka's again.

He turned away. 'I don't know what it is you want me to see.'

'Oh Subbu. Maybe one day it will come to you.'

'What? Why can't you just tell me?'

'There's nothing to tell. It's what you know already.'

'Like what?'

'Have you never noticed? You don't have a father, and I don't have a father.'

'You do have a father. Vallabendran is your father.'

'If he was my father, he wouldn't want to fuck me now, would he?'

Subbu had no answer to that.

'Your father, they say, could look at the positions of the

planets on the day of one's birth, or at the lines on one's palm and tell everything about one's life. He looked at my chart, so he must have known this was going to happen to me. And he must have known what was going to happen to you. You'd think he wouldn't have left us to suffer with only our mothers for support, our selfish, silly mothers. Do you hate your father, Subbu, for leaving you?'

'No, I don't hate him. He must have had his reasons. I only wish I knew what they were.'

'Yes, well, I don't hate Vallabendran, or my real father either. What would be the purpose?'

'You know who your real father is? Did Nagaveni tell you?'

'I figured it out, a long time ago. If you knew where he was, your father, would you go and find him?'

'Don't tell me you know that too?'

'No, I don't know that.'

And so they'd walked slowly side by side all the way to his street. As she turned the corner towards her house and moved out of his sight, the unease that had been a small pulse at the start of their conversation began to throb in earnest. He'd suspected then that something was wrong and yet he'd done nothing. Her setting right of the past, her apologies and her words about his father – what was he to make of all that? He could have run after her. He could have . . . But really, what could he have done?

If only his father was here. Subbu could still conjure up an image very clearly, of a tall, handsome man with skin the colour of ripening wheat, who looked down on him with gentle eyes and said, 'Subbu, my son, my dear son, I am going to do you a grave injustice. But I have responsibilities to others as well, and my duties demand that I must go away from here for a while. It may be for so long that you forget you ever had a father. I have told your mother, she has accepted it, and so must you.'

'But why, Appa?'

'Three reasons, Subbu. Each by itself would not be enough, but the weight of the three together is an unbearable burden that must be discharged.'

'Tell me why! It is not fair.'

'I can't disclose the details, but I will tell you in general terms. First and most important, my presence is a threat to others, innocent of any sin, who would suffer by my being in their vicinity. Second, I have performed an evil act, for which I must perform the requisite expiation so that its effects do not follow me over lifetimes. Third, it is clearly indicated by the position of Rahu in my eleventh house that after my forty-second year, I must roam. It would be detrimental to stay in one place.'

Subbu knew in a secret part of his mind that such a conversation had never really taken place. The reasons his father had given were reasons he himself had made up, reasons to justify in some way his father's actions, and allow Subbu to continue to love and admire the man. This was the version of his father's leaving he'd recalled so often that it had become completely muddled with the reality of events as they'd unfolded.

He no longer even tried to distinguish between the two, the words his flesh-and-blood father had once really spoken and the words he'd only heard in his mind. The voice that spoke to him so gently and with such wisdom, wherever it came from, was the voice of the father he kept with him. This father spoke to him still, and consoled him, long after that ordinary day when he'd been abandoned by the real man.

These conversations that went on inside his head had become a constant and ongoing feature of his inner life. His imagined father, always wise, always tender, seemed to have some separate existence from Subbu himself, inside his own head perhaps, but distant for all that, intangible. How could the thoughts be his own, since they took him so much by surprise, and expressed ideas he himself was incapable of?

Subbu's mother was justly proud of her cooking, and Subbu had grown used to the superior taste of the food she prepared. His father told him, 'You will become a great poet because your mother has trained your tongue. In appreciating her food, you have developed your tastes for what is delicate, refined, balanced. These are the qualities you have grown accustomed to and cannot live without. Words will fall from your tongue with the same qualities, and you will know when harmony is needed and when contrast, when sweetness, when spice. She is your first teacher.

'Let your teachers be the poets who have gone before. Learn by imitating them. The world is waiting to reveal itself to those who care to pay attention. For how many thousands of years had the pouring rain mixed with the red earth of the fields, before the Poet of Red Earth and Pouring Rain saw their mingling as the image of love? Now his words, already more than a thousand years old, will live on for another thousand years.

'All poets sing of love. Because a heart opened by love sees the world afresh. Love itself may be fleeting but in memory it lives on to light the way for many poems. Don't think love brings happiness; in fact, it is the opposite: love brings heartache and tears and more tears. But poets need love, and love needs poets. And if your words are sweet, they will mend torn hearts. I am telling you all this because I want you to be a better man than I am, especially in the realm of love.'

Should his flesh-and-blood father ever return, he would drive this other away, and of the two, it might well be the imagined one who was kinder and more consoling. Would a real father take an interest in his poems and make useful and critical comments? Subbu doubted it very much. But in this situation he longed for the real man, as the imagined being, in light of the strange events in the real world, had lost his efficacy. Now, when he needed advice about the very real disappearance of Kanaka and the appearance of the statue, this imaginary father spoke to him in clichés of what no longer interested him.

He didn't want to think of poems, he didn't want to think of love. He wanted only to find Kanaka.

He walked back to Nagaveni's house. When he entered her street, he heard someone shouting. The wife of Ganapathy, the drummer, was standing and cursing right out in front of the door of the dasi house. That door remained closed, but every other one on the street was open, and all the neighbours were peering out and watching as she flaunted her anger. She took turns shouting at the closed door and at the curious audience. 'That whore Kanaka, she's run off with my husband, hasn't she? Turned into gold! What a story! You know where they are, Nagaveni. Tell me. I'm not a fool.' When she got tired of shouting, she picked up a stone from the street and threw it at the door. 'Come and face me, Nagaveni. Tell the truth. I know what's going on.'

Subbu couldn't enter Nagaveni's house now. He'd have to go home and try again in the morning.

His mother was waiting for him when he reached

home. She said eagerly, 'Did you hear what our neighbour's daughter-in-law is saying? Don't ignore me, Subbu, this will interest you. It has to do with Kanaka.'

'Fine, tell me.'

'The woman was coming back from the river after her bath yesterday, carrying the clothes she'd washed in a bucket, and a pot of water on her head, so she couldn't do more than stand with her mouth open in amazement.'

'About what?'

'Just at the place where the path curves, Durga ran past her, and as she ran, she was saying right out loud, absolutely clearly and unmistakably, "Ka na ka Ka na ka Ka na ka." That too is a miracle, isn't it?'

'Are you saying the girl can now talk?'

'I don't know, I'm just telling you the story that's going around. Maybe she's said one word, so why not more? And why now? All of a sudden.'

'But that means this happened before the statue appeared.'

'Before, after, who cares? It is connected. A girl who can't talk, who's never said a word in all her nine years, suddenly says "Kanaka". And she was all by herself, not attached to Kanaka as she always is. So how do you explain that, Subbu?'

'Well, why don't you just ask Durga? If she can talk, she'll tell you.'

As night descended, Subbu lay down to sleep outside on

the thinnai, still warm from the afternoon sun, and tried to make some sense of all that had happened. No, even the conversation he'd had with Kanaka the evening before her disappearance was not the beginning of the story, nor even were the fights and the lies she'd told. She'd behaved strangely even before that.

Maybe the guava was the beginning. She'd said one day, 'I'm going to the wild guava tree, I think the fruit will be ripe. I'm in a hurry, so you don't come, Subbu. I'll bring some back for you.' He'd been hurt, of course, but he'd tried not to show it. She'd run off, Durga tagging along behind her. Subbu made excuses for Kanaka: she did have many duties, and she could get there much more quickly if he wasn't slowing her down. But such missions were of their own making, the fruit itself hardly worth the effort. So why go at all if not for the companionship and shared adventure? Then later, when she'd given him the guavas as promised, they were pink inside and sweet, while the wild guavas they'd picked before had always been much smaller, white-fleshed and hard. So she'd lied about going to pick fruit. But why? Kanaka hadn't wanted him around, then given herself away with fruit from the market. He had no way of knowing where she really went. How was he to find the beginning of the story, when it had taken place outside his line of vision?

If only Durga really could talk. She'd been with Kanaka

that day, and every other day too. But she was immune to blandishment, ignoring slaps, sweets, and most of what went on around her, responding if at all only to Kanaka. She sat where Kanaka made her sit without making a sound, hardly moving, staring intently at the ground in front of her or at the bark of a tree or even at a wall, as if the whole universe was contained within it.

Other than her singing, which no one had expected of her, and which she'd never been taught and did only when it pleased her to do so, she had one more skill. As she walked behind Kanaka or as she sat somewhere, she might suddenly bend to pick up something. The objects that attracted her eye were not always precious. It might turn out to be a key someone had lost months ago or the screw of a gold earring or a silver chain that had broken and had slipped unseen from someone's neck, but it could just as well be a bead or a piece of glass or an iridescent feather from a rooster. It had been Nagaveni's habit to collect these bits and pieces in an old Parry's biscuit tin with a faded pink-cheeked baby on the lid. When anyone lost anything of the kind Durga might pick up, they would go to Nagaveni's house and rummage through the objects there. If they found what they had lost, they might choose to give her a few coins depending on the object's value.

Everyone in the village knew of her condition, and if, as

once or twice happened, Kanaka had left her in one spot and forgotten to collect her, someone would run and tell Nagaveni as only she, other than Kanaka, was permitted to touch her and take her home.

Tonight I will dream of Kanaka, Subbu thought to himself, and tomorrow I will force Durga to talk. I will make her tell me what she knows.

Jackals were howling somewhere along the river. I could hear them snarling at one another. He wondered how many there were to make so much noise. Perhaps there was an injured calf in the woods. Or perhaps the Tombans had put out bait to bring them there. They ate the filthy animals. Subbu couldn't imagine anything more disgusting, unless it was the rats, also a part of their diet. He heard from the next house the wail of a child, and the stern voice of the father, then crying dissolving into stifled sobs and finally quiet except for the incessant hum of the night insects.

In the morning, Subbu's first task was to examine the contents of the box. He asked Nagaveni for it, pretending to have lost the silver cap of his pen. At first, nothing struck him as being unusual or different. But then he noticed that three items were of a particular kind. One was a small silver arm, another a silver eye, the third a hand-length silver spear such as men used to pierce their cheeks during the thai pusam festival. These were objects associated with vows and offerings. Of course, they might be from the banks of the river, where he knew Kanaka went regularly to bathe, with Durga in tow. But the silver spear at least was something a man had lost, not likely to be found at the spot where women bathed. He wondered if there was some other place they could have been dropped and then found by Durga.

He couldn't check that part of the river anyway, he'd only get into trouble with the women. But it would do no harm to go up to the point where the neighbour's daughter-in-law had seen Durga running and saying 'Kanaka'. Once he neared the curve, he walked slowly looking for anything that might give a clue as to what had made Durga speak. But all Subbu could see was trees. A tree with a deeply fissured bark formed eyes where branches had broken, and they stared back at him. Thick creepers striped yellow on green and as big as elephant ears climbed high and twisted into the branches. He stood in one place, turning his body slightly as if moving through the minute positions on the face of a clock, taking the time to examine the ground on either side of the path. Before he'd even moved to the one o'clock position, he noticed something incongruous – a long, dried frond of a coconut palm lay at the base of a tree. But there were no coconut trees in this part of the jungle and the more he looked at the frond, the more it looked artfully placed. He moved it, and there seemed the faintest hint of a path, a thin ridge of stony red earth showing through the brown leaves in the patches of dappled sunlight that filtered through the dense canopy of green. He made his way along it, behind a strangler fig, plunging through thorny shrubs, bending under low branches of young trees and creepers. The smell of humus rose to his nostrils in the hot air. The ground all around was a thick carpet of dried leaves in all stages of disintegration. When he looked up, he saw the filigree of black leaves and branches edged in light. Around him, the leaves rustled as he parted them, in every shade of green, in shapes large and small, smooth and serrated. Here and there, the ghostly petals of elephant apple flowers lay undisturbed and unremembered, though their simple understated beauty pierced him as one more aspect of the world he could never share with anyone. Above, a weaver bird he couldn't see said 'which? which? which?' and another bird responded with the same question. When Subbu smelled the heady fragrance of wild jasmine, and saw the thick, twisting creepers climbing up into the branches of kondrai trees, he realized he was moving through what poets called mullai thinai, the landscape of separation. He'd never thought of the five thinais as real before. They were merely conceits, poetic devices, conventions within which the woodland, with kondrai, kaya and mullai, signals the pain of being abandoned after union. But it was not so, it was very real. These trees and roots and leaves vibrated within him, as the plucked string on the veena causes the sympathetic strings to vibrate. Sweating from the heat and the exertion of walking on uneven ground, fighting his way over tree roots and decaying branches, he was walking through the landscape of his own mood.

When he came all of a sudden to a clearing where he could make out the stone edge of the old temple tank, he realized where he was. Years ago, before his illness, he and Kanaka had roamed freely, exploring the whole of the village and its surroundings. At that time, though the tank was already dried up and disused, farmers drove carts up to it from the main road to collect the rich silt that covered the bottom. He and Kanaka had always approached it from that direction, following the track made by the bullock carts. Long since, the silt had been all used up, so even the ruts etched by the cartwheels were completely overgrown.

Subbu tried to walk around the outside perimeter of the tank but it was covered in a thick growth of thorny subabul shrubs, and in several places the granite walls had fallen in, so he gave up. He sat on the top step and rested. Durga could have found the ritual objects here, where in times past, when the tank had been full, devotees would have bathed before going to the temple to make their vows. He'd bring Durga here tomorrow. Maybe her response would tell him something. Maybe she really would talk.

The next morning, Subbu positioned himself by the back gate of Nagaveni's house, when he knew she would still be at the temple. Word of the miracle had quickly spread, and every scheduled puja was crowded with people who wanted darshan of the golden devadasi. Nagaveni played her part with pride.

When he heard the dasi girls go out and take their place on the veranda, where they would sit and gossip and watch the world go by, he entered quietly and looked for Durga. She sat in a corner in the back courtyard, where the well was, in her usual trance. 'You have to help me, Durga. I don't know what to do. No one else cares. You have to tell me what you know.' She made no response, gave no sign that she'd understood, or even heard what he said. He yanked her to a standing position and dragged her after him out to the lane. Seeing that she put up no struggle but followed him willingly, he let go of her wrist. She stood there. Tentatively, Subbu took her hand. She didn't pull away. They walked together, she not seeming by any overt sign to know where she was going, but not struggling to get away either, as she had done in the past when anyone other than Kanaka or Nagaveni had tried to control her.

When they finally reached the tank, Subbu was disappointed. Durga did nothing, just stood and stared silently as she always did. The stone steps along one side were uneven but stable, so Subbu took her hand again and made his way with her down to the bottom. Durga stopped when he stopped. She said nothing. Subbu let go of her hand and she sat down. He left her sitting, staring, and walked all the way around along the inside perimeter. He could see nothing that told him where Kanaka could be now, or what she was doing when she'd come here, if indeed she had come here.

When he had circled back to Durga, she was pulling at something that was pushed tight into the gap between two stones of the step. It was yellow silk, all crumpled up into a tight ball, and covered in dirt. He took it from Durga and shook it out. A skirt. Kanaka's skirt. Subbu remembered the fight they'd had over it. One evening, he'd asked her innocently, 'Why did you change the yellow pavadai you were wearing earlier? It looked so pretty.' She'd got angry for no reason. 'I didn't wear a yellow skirt, I've worn this green one all day.' 'You were wearing a yellow pavadai with small silver bottus, I remember.' 'Well, it must have been a dream you had, because I don't even have a pavadai like that.' He'd stubbornly insisted he'd seen her in a yellow skirt. She'd called him an idiot and blind. He hadn't known what to make of her adamant denial, he'd felt so sure of what he'd seen. And so they'd fought. Now here it was, with a round stain of dried blood on it, the size of a betel nut. He held the skirt up in front of Durga and asked her, 'What happened to Kanaka? Who was with her here?' Nothing in her expression changed. 'Durga, please,' begged Subbu, 'tell me what you know. You are the only one who can help me. Please.' But she said nothing.

Subbu had found the place where the silver tokens of offering could have come from, and the skirt with the blood confirmed that Kanaka had been here. He knew the meaning of the blood, and that explained why Kanaka had been so adamant in denying that she'd ever worn it. But who had been here with her? Could it really have been Ganapathy as his wife believed?

Laboriously he climbed up the steps, leading Durga back the way they'd come. When they reached the point where the jungle track met the path to the river, Durga began to sing a padam, but the words in Telegu didn't tell Subbu anything he didn't already know – Kanaka had a lover.

When she's with you, shouldn't I be embarrassed?

When you and she talk in private, shouldn't I stay outside the gate?

When you two lie together, covered in her shawl, shouldn't I play dice?

He'd seen Ratna dance that padam. She'd mimed all those things she'd observed as the reluctant third party to her lover's love play with another woman – the sly disrobing, the pinching of nipples, the sounds they made, like the cooing of doves, and even more explicit descriptions of lovemaking, the woman getting on top, or standing and climbing him like a tree, or turning her back to his front, or her mouth to his private parts and his mouth to hers, positions to which she alluded in a language of hand gestures that her patrons well understood. Ratna hadn't been to the temple since the statue had appeared there. Later, Subbu would go and search her out. Surely she would want to know the real reason for her sister's disappearance.

A few days later, Subbu took the winding footpath between fields and open scrubland to Ratna's house, but as he walked he became less and less sure of Ratna's response. Mostly she seemed indifferent to Kanaka, but at times he'd seen her behave with open hostility. She might keep quiet, if doing so was detrimental to her younger sister's interests. What if she'd had a hand in Kanaka's disappearance? At the same time, Ratna took great pride in her lineage, praised by poets over centuries. She would not take kindly to the suggestion that a miracle within her family was impossible. What would he answer if she asked, with perfect justification, 'What business is this of yours?' She might mock him, evade his questions, prevaricate with a flow of witty double entendres. After all, she was a devadasi.

When he arrived at the house, it was even grander than he remembered. He steeled himself to open the gate and proceed along the path lined with every flower of the season.

Ratna's maid was sitting at the top of the steps leading to the wide, pillared veranda, one leg tucked under her, the other hanging down and swinging. She was winnowing rice in a fan-shaped muram, tossing the grains up with a practised flick of the wrists to release the chaff into the breeze, and shaking them when they fell back down to bring stones to the surface. The chaff hung for a moment like gold dust in the morning sun before dispersing, as the rice, white and shaped like jasmine buds, fell back into the winnow with a murmur. Hypnotized by the dance of her bare ankle and slender arms, Subbu watched her without saying a word. Even the servants of devadasis were pretty, neat and well dressed. The woman was wearing a silk blouse to do household chores! The maid took no notice of him, and remained intent on her task, interrupting the rhythmic toss – toss – shake, toss – toss – shake only to bend and pick out small stones.

Without turning to look at him, she suddenly said, 'How long are you going to stand there with your mouth hanging open? Come on, state your business.'

'I want to talk to Ratnavalli,' Subbu answered, using the most respectful form of address.

'Oh dear. I don't need that fine way of talking, I'm only the maid.'

Subbu didn't know what to say to that, and made no reply.

The maid put the winnow to one side, and placed both legs across the top step.

'You'll have to say, 'Lift your legs so I can climb up,' and she giggled. It was a line from a rude joke often told in koothus. Subbu understood its double meaning and flushed.

'I need to see your mistress. It's important.'

'Oh really? Is she expecting you?'

'No,' Subbu admitted.

'Well, she's still sleeping. She made love until dawn. Oh, the tricks they got up to . . . Her lord was thoroughly charmed. No wonder she's exhausted. Covered in sweat and bite marks. And when she does wake, she won't want to see a cripple first thing, that's inauspicious. But it is auspicious to see a Brahmin. Hmmmmm. You're a contradiction. Anyway, when she calls me to prepare her bath, I can tell her you're waiting. Come, sit up here.'

Subbu sat down on the step below her.

'My mistress has no appetite, she would rather starve than eat anything ordinary. That's just the way she is. So I'm cooking this rice for her. Thooya Malli.' The maid picked up the winnow again and held it for him to inhale the scent, then sniffed it herself. 'The smell as it cooks makes your mouth water. I have to make delicacies. Oh, there, she's getting up. Yes, mistress, I'm coming.' Her ears, tuned to Ratna's voice, caught her summons before Subbu heard anything. She rose quickly and entered the house, closing the door behind her, but not completely. Subbu could hear her talking in respectful tones but could not make out her words. Then came the clang of brass vessels, the pouring of water and splashing. After some time, she came out again.

'All that waiting has got you nowhere. She won't see you after all. She's not well. Her friend is visiting.'

Subbu looked confused.

'The river is flowing.'

When she saw that Subbu still didn't understand, she said, 'It's her time of the month. She can't converse with you now when she's unclean. For her it can be very bad. Sometimes she'll bleed and bleed until the midwife has to be called. Come back in a few days.'

But before he could do so, the body was found.

In the dream he's standing with Kanaka, back to back. That much is a fragment of the memory that has never left him. But they are not the age they were when they had stood like that. They are their present age, fifteen, when the surge of blood between his legs has become a familiar phenomenon. The withered leg never enters his dreams, so he is whole and standing straight and tall when he feels her curved bum pressed against his. In the dream no other beings exist. They are not in the garden, or they could have been – it's hard to say, the focus of all sensation so concentrated on his back that he can't tell what is there in front of his eyes. In the dream he stands like this for a long time. Kanaka doesn't say anything. He hears very loudly the *drip, drip, drip* of water falling on the packed earth. He doesn't feel her braid. Instead he feels wet, matted hair against his bare skin and water trickling down his spine. That is why he turns.

In the dream he doesn't know what he's going to see, he feels the same shock each time he dreams it. She is naked. He'd wanted to see her naked, imagined it, desired it with sick longing so many times. But as always, his desires regarding Kanaka have been thwarted, getting what he's asked for without getting what he wants. Now all he wants is to have never seen her like this, but it's too late. What he's seen can never be unseen.

Water drips from her body, making a puddle all around her. It doesn't stop dripping, it's dripping out of her. The beloved face is still her face, it is still Kanaka. That is what hurts the most. Only one eye is open, the other is half closed. Her skin, soaked with the water, is thickened and swollen like a peel. It has lost all colour, now a mottled grey. In places – her hands and feet and the round balls of her shoulders and knees – the skin has split open and curled away, revealing the layer underneath. This is the moment he knows he is dreaming, which is also the precise moment he wakes up, too soon for the dream to tell him anything. The image of the skin peeled away from the bone of her shoulder – that was real, it wasn't only a detail of a nightmare. That was how it had been when they pulled her out of the well, and laid her all wet on the earth.

There is something on the periphery of his vision, or something that should be there, but isn't. He needs to turn his head, in the dream. But who can control their dreams? He's just about to see it when he wakes up.

For a long time, he dreamed that dream every night. He's almost choking when he wakes, the thought he'd been thinking sliding away into an abyss before he can say what it was. Every time he has the same feeling, of both presence and absence, the word on the tip of the tongue, but unsayable.

Subbu knows he'll always be at the end of the story, trying to claw his way back to the beginning through the heap of ashes that is the past. Every day – every moment – that goes by adds more to the pile, so he's always further and further away. But of this he's certain: whatever he knows cannot be unknown. This gives him some relief.

The Grandmother

The old lady smelled smoke. It seemed to be coming from inside her, the fever burning up her brittle bones. Her body under the thin sheet lay in disarray, like a puppet with broken strings. No one had come in this morning to open her curtains or spoon-feed her the thin rice gruel she lived on. The pale morning light entered the room only as a thin border of silver along the edge of the dark curtains.

She wasn't thinking about dying. She was thinking about how miserable her daughter-in-law would be – even in death she'd have the upper hand. She almost laughed out loud, she was so pleased with herself. Her reasons for hating Devayani were vague and meaningless: her accent, her oh-so-holy airs, the way she pursed her lips, the saris she wore – but these were only the words she used to justify the feeling that came before reasons needed to be invented for it.

Carried out of her room so rarely now, she had become used to living through the lives of others. Ever since Indra had come back from his college and resumed his daily morning visit to her, sat beside her on the bed holding her hand and telling her of his beloved, she had been overtaken by feelings, moods, sensations, as if she had become a young girl again – no, had become that girl, for her own girlhood had included no such interludes. When she married her husband, Indra's grandfather, he already had a big belly, bowed skinny legs and breath so fetid her eyes watered when he panted over her. Whatever incidents Indra told her had become long, intimate scenes that she watched as if looking through a keyhole, or from above, as if perched in a tree, or even sometimes, from the inside, as if she was covered in the girl's skin. She felt no shame. It wasn't her grandson's touch, it was the god Indra, always on the prowl for earthly beauties, who unloosed her hair and spread it like a peacock's tail behind her naked body. She has no sense of decorum, no modesty. She lets him look at her, she looks at him. She presses up against him, she writhes in his arms. Tender young girl, strong young boy, how beautiful they looked with the sunlight falling on their naked bodies.

She felt the warm flow of urine between her legs and the sting of it on her bedsores. Then the stink. So what, she thought to herself, this is my body and this is what my body does. Anyway, this too would make Devayani angry. She would have to bend over this stinking body and search in the dirty bed to find the key. But the key was gone. And all the precious objects it once had the power to unlock? Gone, Devayani, gone. The edge of light seeped away from the window and gathered into moving, dancing shapes in front of her. Was she already dead? Were flames licking her body? Nothing could clean her now but the fire.

Vallabendran

Vallabendran dismounted from his horse at the gate, and cursed. 'Where the hell is the lazy durwah? Either I find him sleeping, or not here altogether. Leaving the gate open for anyone to enter! I'll skin him alive.' The mare whinnied. 'Quiet, Moti, I'm not angry with you.' He looped the reins over the gatepost and left the horse there with a pat on the neck, saying, 'Stay here, dearest, the groom will come and take you to the stable. He will feed you.' He walked towards the stables along the side of the house but then changed his mind and headed to the grand front entrance, along the broad, tree-lined avenue, wanting nothing more than to go quietly to his bedroom and sleep. 'I'm the raja. Who is there to question me? I don't need to sneak into my own house.' Just then the gatekeeper appeared, running towards him, saying, 'Sorry, Raja,' and some other words, but Vallabendran didn't listen. 'Shut up, you black dog, and don't let me catch you missing from your post again. I'm too tired to beat you right now. See that the groom attends to Moti.' He kept on walking. The tall ashoka trees which lined the carriageway had been planted by his father. Now, in the hot season, the dark green spear-shaped leaves were covered by a fine coating of red dust. The fountain was empty of water, the bottom caked in algae baked grey and black by the summer sun. Vallabendran walked up the marble steps and between the Indo-Saracenic pillars of the open front porch. No servant rushed towards him to relieve him of his boots. He'd been awake the whole night, and now his head was throbbing with the incessant rhythmic swell of his own blood. He needed quiet. He needed to lie down. He needed to take off all his clothes and sleep, with only the fans moving the air gently over his naked body.

But the place he entered was not the one he'd left, quiet and calm; it was in turmoil, servants running around like ants in an anthill that's been kicked. A chicken with its head cut off lay on the granite floor, feathers soaked in a pool of its own blood. The knife with the curved iron blade that had done the work lay where it had been flung. He could hear the sound of chanting, smell camphor burning. Strangely, his own servants ignored his entrance, as if the tasks they were on the way to perform were a matter of life and death, more important than his presence. He staggered to a chair and sat down, too surprised to even shout at the boy who was running from the kitchen across the foyer to the family wing of the house. He needed a drink. Then he'd figure out what on earth was going on. But first a drink. He struggled to his feet again and headed towards the parlour containing the liquor cabinet. Janardana, his brother-in-law, carrying a stack of towels like a servant late for his duties, ran past him and he shouted, 'Janardana! Tell me what in god's name is going on!' but his brother-in-law waved him off and went on his way.

Devayani, his own wife, almost rushed right past him too, but then she saw it was him and stopped. He was shocked at her face, the reddened eyes, the lids all swollen from crying.

'You! Did you once think of us while in the company of your whores? Did wife or son come to mind even once? When I need you, you're nowhere to be found. Why bother to come home now.'

'What's happened? Is it Indra?' The sound of his son's name brought the blood pounding to his head.

'You've brought this curse on us. Your actions. Your debauchery. Your unnatural lust.'

'Just tell me what has happened.'

'Your son is lying unconscious in the next room. That's all. He's hardly breathing. But why should you care, as long as you are being serviced! That is the most important thing, that your prick should be inside some harlot.'

'Don't curse like a fishwife. Tell me. What happened?'

'You planted only the one seed in me, in all these twenty-six years of our marriage. Now that poor child is paying the price for your sins. If the boy dies, I will walk out from here and never come back. I'll put on orange robes, I'll renounce the world.'

'For god's sake! Will you tell me what happened?'

'We've been looking for him ever since his horse came back in the night without him. Finally the men going to the fields beside the mango orchard found him in the ditch. He was unconscious and they carried him here. The vaid said it was a scorpion's bite, and put on a poultice of herbs, but he worsened. He was hardly breathing. I sent for the white doctor. It was three hours before he could get here. I sent a servant to Ratna's house; no one was there. I had to do everything myself. And now you show up, smelling of wine and scented hair. If the boy dies, I swear on my son's head, you'll never see me again. You can spend all your time enjoying the cacophony of your whores.'

Vallabendran strode ahead of his wife into his son's room. Indra lay on the bed, silent and still. The priestess from the Mariamman temple was shaking and shivering in a trance, saying unintelligible words and waving a small broom made of grass fronds over the boy's body, from head to feet, again and again. On the floor, in the corner, a temporary shrine had been set up. In front of the black stone that represented Mariamman, goddess of diseases, a bowl held the chicken's blood. The smell of it mixed with the jasmine and camphor.

The doctor rose from the chair beside the bed.

'Raja.' He put his hand out and Vallabendran took it. 'I am Doctor Burke. Let us go out and talk for a minute.'

'Well? How is he? What can you tell me?'

'His heartbeat is irregular, that is the most dangerous sign, and what I am watching closely. The heart has undergone some swelling. He is unconscious, but that is not a bad thing, not at all. Otherwise he would be in great pain. The poison enters the blood and then spreads through the body, causing unspeakable agony. It will take some days before it works its way out. There is not much that can be done for him. He'd had a good deal to drink, your boy. What we are seeing now may be some of the effects of alcohol in conjunction with the venom. Let him rest and we'll keep checking his heartbeat, that's all we can do for the moment. And all the chanting and waving of incense – it won't do him a bit of harm, and it will keep his mother occupied. She's worked herself up into quite a state, so it may help to let her have her way on that front. The vaid has mashed up a good mess of neem leaves and turmeric root and gingelly oil. I've left that as it is; for all I know, that may be what sees him through the night. The old vaid's had more experience with scorpions than I have. I'm sure that's a thought that's occurred to you. Well, I've seen enough to know what helps and what's no better than writing on water.'

'So he's not going to die.' The expression in his voice brought the doctor's eyes to his face. He paused and answered the question he'd been asked and not the one he thought he'd heard.

'It happens, of course, but rarely. Children, usually, because of their small size. But it does happen, so I don't intend to relax my vigil yet. The edema – swelling – of the heart cannot be taken lightly. I've seen all kinds of strange effects; every scorpion has a different poison, and they sting not once, but again and again, six, seven, eight times. No doubt your son got a hefty dose. Sometimes there is temporary blindness, paralysis, difficulty in speaking, best be prepared for that. It's frightening, of course, but it generally goes away in a month or so.'

'A month!'

'A moment ago all you wanted was that he not die. Now go on, go and console your wife.'

But Vallabendran did not go to Devayani. The words she'd spoken to him still rankled. 'How dare she! Let her think the worst.' He went straight to his room and rang the bell for his manservant.

'Bring me a whisky, right now. And tell Janardana to come to my room, immediately.' He said to himself, 'Let's see him defend this conduct of his sister.'

'Yes, my lord.' The servant bowed low and backed out of the room.

Two attendants came running in to undress him. He stared at himself in the mirror as they removed the fine cotton shirt embroidered all over with leaves and flowers, and the trousers in British style. He was a tall man, and he admired his strong legs and bull-like chest. His waist had thickened but other than that he was as handsome and powerful as he'd ever been. Fifty is a fine age for a man. He took the two ends of the lungi from the boys, and wrapped it, saying to them as they left, 'Tell Thambi to bring the hookah along with the whisky.'

He paced the room as he waited for his brother-in-law.

'Brother-in-law! You are back! Where did you go last night? You weren't at Ratna's place.'

'That's no one's business but my own, but just for your information, Ratna has taken a vow for my health and gone on a pilgrimage. She left this morning. Maybe she had some premonition of this evil that's befallen Indra.'

'She didn't tell me anything of such a plan.'

'Does she tell you everything?'

'When will she be back?'

'Who knows. And what concern is it of yours? Keep your mind on your own affairs.' He directed his pent-up anger at Janardana and his voice rose. 'Who gave you permission to hang around Ratna as you do? Visiting her late at night – I don't want to hear again of such improprieties, brother-in-law, and I will hear, don't discount it. People know who rules here.'

'Whatever you say. I thought . . . but never mind, I'm yours to command.' Janardana changed the subject, while maintaining his obsequious tone. 'How worried my sister was, with son sick and husband nowhere to be found. She feared the worst, let me tell you. I told her, "Don't worry, the boy has Scorpio ascendant, he won't come to harm," but she wouldn't listen.'

'Your sister has uttered words to me that no wife has the right to know, much less to say. I controlled myself, but I could have slapped her, and no one could have blamed me. She has no right to meddle in my affairs!'

'Meddle? Raja!' Janardana settled himself on the settee like a well-fed cat. 'When I brought her here as a girl, to be your bride, Nagaveni was already installed in your heart and in your bed. Devayani understood her sphere, and she kept to it. When Ratna replaced her own mother, what did my sister do? Welcomed her, made room for her at all ceremonial occasions.'

'So? She kept quiet all these years, but now suddenly she has plenty to say!'

'Devayani is the mother of your son. If she said something she shouldn't have, it is only from a surfeit of worry and heartache over Indra's condition. Surely you can forgive her under these circumstances.'

'Who told her about my plans? If it is you, Janardana, fomenting trouble, I'll throw you out on the street.'

'Me? After all your generosity to a poor good-for-nothing with nowhere else to go? No, no, it wasn't me. Can't you guess who spilled the beans?'

'Don't play your silly games. I'm not in the mood.'

'Well, I can't say for certain, but I do know who came here out of the blue and stayed with your wife all alone in her room for some time. I don't know what was said of course – how could I? But my guess is that you and your plans were the main topic of discussion. What other business would Nagaveni have with my sister?'

'Nagaveni came here? When?'

'Look, it is no big secret. And Nagaveni knows you better than anyone. She wouldn't hesitate to beg Devayani to put a stop to it. If my sister knows your plans, she got the news straight from the source.'

'You better explain the situation to your sister. Tell her I am doing nothing wrong.'

'Who am I to say right or wrong to you, Raja? But this

does not look proper. The girl's called you Appa from the moment she could talk.'

'That is Nagaveni up to her tricks. She taught the baby to say that, just to wheedle money from me, for jewels and dresses, this ceremony and that ceremony. I hardly saw the girl. One doesn't keep a devadasi to have cosy family gatherings.'

'But that's exactly my point. You've done a father's duty to her nevertheless, and now you can't turn around and fuck her, without causing talk. Find yourself some other young girl. Why must it be Kanaka?'

Vallabendran was not given to self-analysis. He hadn't considered whether his plans for Kanaka were right or wrong, good or bad, or affected those around him in any way. He was used to all his desires being satisfied, and this was no different. Except that desire itself seemed to have left him. He felt a vague dissatisfaction, an irritation with the world. More and more often these days all Ratna's skills were useless. He remained as limp as an overripe banana.

He wanted to feel the old surge of desire, what he'd felt in those first heady days of his relationship with Nagaveni. Nothing could have stopped him then. He'd been a young man, hardly older than Indra was now. And how beautiful Nagaveni had been. No wonder he'd had little energy to spare for Devayani. Once he'd done his duty, given her a male child, he'd lost what little interest he'd had in his wife. She knew nothing of the tricks Nagaveni used to bring him again and again to the state that the sages compared to nirvana. Even now, all these years later, he was affected by the memory of a banal but potent image: the way Nagaveni took the stem of the betel leaf and bit it off with her sharp white teeth and then blew it out to one side through half-opened lips showing the tip of her tongue, almost a kiss. She cleaned the leaf by brushing it back and forth along her thigh, looking at him all the while and letting the pallav of her sari fall just enough so that he could see the top curve of her breasts pushed together by the tight choli. She could read his mind, light the fire in him.

He took one of the roses out of the bowl beside his bed. The petals were a deep, fleshy pink, like Ratna's tongue or the inside of her lower lip when she pouted at not getting her way. And Nagaveni had trained Ratna well. All those little tricks she had to make him lose control. He flung the rose across the room.

A great tiredness overcame Vallabendran, so pervasive that he sat down on the carved rosewood bed and let himself fall backwards. Now his eyelids closed of their own accord. Janardana's disembodied voice came to him as the echo of words spoken into a dark cave.

'How can you go to sleep with your feet so dirty? I will

wash them for you. Where have you been to get mud past the top of your boots?' Then there came the sound of water being poured from a pitcher, and soon a wet cloth was being rubbed on the soles of his feet and between his toes. The voice continued soothing and consoling him, as the towel moved to the tops of his feet and his calves. 'Don't disturb yourself, you're tired.'

God, he was tired. Disembodied hands massaged his calves. 'Your muscles are all tight. Relax.'

The erection came of its own accord, when he was beyond needing it or wanting it. 'What appetites you still have. You're a man among men, Vallabendran.' He could feel the fingers but couldn't remember whose fingers they were. So maybe this is all he needed, relaxation that was almost total, and a skilled hand, not attached to any body. Or a virgin's blood, that was known to be a sure-fire cure. He would visit the nearby villages and look for a young girl. A virgin, that was what he needed to restore his virility. Any kind of alliance with Kanaka was now out of the question. Vallabendran entered completely into the sensation the hand was creating, and then seamlessly into sleep.

Indra

I used to be the spoiled little prince, carried through the village on a palanquin on every special occasion or sitting atop an elephant hired for festivals, or riding my proud little Deccani pony or pedalling a BSA bicycle sent all the way from England. Then I was packed away to boarding school, where I learned quickly that I was someone of no consequence after all, neither the tallest nor the strongest nor the quickest of wit, worthy of no special consideration as the son of a raja in name only among the sons of kings and ministers and even Englishmen. I picked up the correct English accent and the correct way of doing perfectly ordinary things that up to then I'd done entirely wrongly. I learned to sit without shaking my legs constantly, to properly wield knife and fork and chew soundlessly, mouth closed, with the requisite indifference to taste, to discharge my snot into a handkerchief and carry it around in my pocket, to brilliantine my hair to just the right degree, neither too little nor too much, to stop plucking my eyebrows and wearing kohl, to stride rather than walk and to shake hands with the degree of firmness deemed properly masculine. These lessons were reinforced when I went to England, where I had to go if I was to join that class of persons best designed to rule: Indian in blood and colour, but English in tastes, in opinions, in morals and in intellect.

They have a saying, 'Even a cat may look at a king', and it's quite true over there, not like our streets, where some people are so low that they should not look up and meet another person's gaze, and even their shadows should not fall on someone of higher status. At first I hated being a nobody instead of claiming my status as a zamindar's son – the tepid tea brought up to my room by a serving man who wasn't afraid to show that he looked down on me, the slimy eggs in the dining hall, the cold, clammy room with mouldering walls. I wanted to come home, but it was my mother, my sweet, indulgent mother, who wouldn't allow it. I think she understood that India was changing and if I grew up to be a man just like my father there would be no place in it for me.

The English boys in my boarding school might have thought very highly of themselves, but they'd been on my patch, I'd known how to handle them. In England it was different – I'd entered their territory. Their innate sense of superiority was insidious and permeated their interactions with all races, especially 'baboos', as they called us, which was too close to 'baboons' for my liking. A man with a black face practising a different religion was reason enough for an Englishman to treat him as a brute. They spoke only the one language, but dismissed my command of English, one of the four languages I speak, as nothing more than a gift for fluency common to all Orientals. My studiousness won me no admirers, paired as it was with the lack of a proper masculine interest in cricket, cricket and nothing but cricket. They considered Hindus to be horribly decadent, given to all sorts of barbarism, and if they didn't say so to our faces, they certainly implied it.

Once I was sitting in the college library reading my book in front of the fire, when a boy at another desk said, 'Damn, I'm out of cigarettes,' and started to leave to get some. 'Here,' I said, opening my silver cigarette case and holding it out to him, 'take one of mine.' He hesitated for only a moment, just an infinitesimally longer pause than was natural, and took one, saying, 'Thanks. It's a noxious habit, isn't it? I should really give it up.' He took my cigarette back to his desk, but he didn't smoke it. That kind of thing happened all the time.

There were other forms their prejudices took, harder to understand or explain. A boy invited me for a weekend at his house so we could indulge our shared passion for chess. To save him embarrassment, I pretended not to notice when at dinner his mother treated me with barely disguised disdain. So imagine my amazement when she entered my room that night and knelt at my bedside. She seemed to need both for her pleasure, first my abasement, then hers. The next morning at breakfast, when another guest expressed an interest in applying for a job in the Colonial Service, she said loudly enough for me to overhear, 'I wouldn't if I were you. A bloody climate. Primitive people. In a year's time, you'll be sitting in a cowshed in the back of beyond, wondering what the hell you did it for. The East is marvellously interesting for going back. But for going forward, it is nothing.' There were further insults about the effeminate Asiatic races, but that, I understood by then, was her idea of foreplay. I got used to Englishwomen from the housemaid classes to the highest offering themselves to me because I was a 'prince', and felt no compunction to disabuse them of that notion.

I never got used to the temperature, or the lack of light, and everything I touched was cold and damp, even my own extremities, even the women who'd come to me for warmth. I learned to keep a certain distance from other Indians as much as from the British. Many of my countrymen seemed to agree with what we were being taught, that a natural order had been established, with white rulers over the brown ruled, so I went with reluctance when a fellow student invited me to a talk at the London India Society. That's where finally I heard a different story. There were some among us who saw nothing natural in the British imposing their will upon Indians and weren't happy to silently endure as England drained our coffers to enrich its own, to the tune of forty million pounds a year. If there was poverty, misery and famine in India, they said, Britain was the reason.

But however poor India was, it was hypocritical of the British to hold it against us given the kind of poverty to be witnessed in the East End of London. Emaciated men and women hardly recognizable as human picked up and ate what even animals would turn away from in our villages. And on the same street, side by side, the most gorgeously dressed women displayed every luxury.

The speaker at the society said that thousands of years ago our sages were pondering philosophical questions while the white man had yet to become aware that such problems even existed. Was it true that Pythagoras had travelled to India to be instructed by Brahmins? I didn't care to verify the claim, but I appreciated the underlying sentiment, that I had reason to hold my head high, as a representative of a lofty culture.

I admired those who wanted to throw the British out of India, but I had no such heroic intentions myself. If they were the bathwater, some of my own rights and privileges were, surely, the baby that would be thrown out with them, so I didn't trust my own nerve. Meanwhile, I prepared for the examination to enter the Indian Civil Service, which had to be written in London. I studied hard, but like most Indians who tried, I failed. So, after four years in England, I came back to India, still my father's son, but also more than that. I had lost my devotion to social custom, and the grip of religion, never tight, had been completely broken. I recognized the cruelty of some practices I'd seen as normal and I could criticize, with an eye to improvement, my country's neglect of modern ways, our inattention to the demands of simple hygiene and proper sanitation. I wanted to move forward rather than dwell on some glorious past.

I saw her for the first time when I'd driven my father's new motor car from the port in Madras to the village where he was attending a cousin's wedding. Appa wanted to show it off, but the roads were so bad and I'd got lost so often that I'd arrived the morning after the ceremony. I drove into the stable area and parked, and then went to the outside tap to wash up before meeting the family.

When I came back, a girl was standing on the running board of the car, peering in through the front window. 'Hey you! Stop that!' I shouted, and she turned, startled, and stepped off, backing away slowly. When I saw her face, the angry words about to spill from my mouth somehow turned into a mumbling apology. She watched my expression change with laughing eyes and smiled, so that a dimple showed in one cheek. Not bold exactly, but she wasn't shy either. 'I was just looking for my sister,' she said. 'I've never seen a motor before. I haven't broken anything.' I wanted to say, 'Go ahead, do what you like with my car, I'll stand here and watch,' but the Tamil language deserted me. Anyway, that's not the kind of thing one can say out loud, so I stuttered, fighting for control of my tongue.

I must have known, deep down, that she wasn't a family girl; no properly brought up young female of my acquaintance, or even a cousin, would have looked so directly at me and spoken so freely. I'd been to whores, and she was nothing like that either, simply dressed in pavadai and dhavani, with a refined and elegant accent and using the Tanjore style of address, the sweetest form of Tamil. A pretty, *very* pretty, young girl with a certain air about her, not a Brahmin, no, not royalty, no, but it never occurred to me that she was a nautch girl or anyone of ill repute. Just then a voice called from the front of the house: 'Kanaka! Ratna! Priya! Kamini! We've found Durga! Let's go.' She turned to leave, and I said, 'Wait! Which one are you?' 'Guess,' she said, and ran off.

I followed her into the house, but by the time I'd greeted

various relatives and made my apologies for turning up so late, she was gone. I tried to inquire discreetly as to who that girl might have been. Even when they told me about the nautch, I didn't make the connection. Amma and her entourage had to be packed into their various carriages and sent off while Appa and I drove behind in the car. We made our way along the one metalled road, lined with tamarind trees, where everyone we passed stopped to stare and wave, talking about what I would do now that I was back. There were men Appa wanted me to meet and reports he wanted me to read about our estate and the villages within our control. 'The British repose faith in some members of our class and not in others,' he said, 'and it depends on how you speak, how you hold your whisky, how you wear your hair, how you flick your lighter open. This is what I sent you to England to learn, and so you have. You've read some books, that's good, but hardly relevant.'

He wanted me to capitalize on my time in London by setting off for Madras right away, but Amma wouldn't agree to let me go. 'He is my only son, whom I haven't set eyes on for four years. I want to keep him close for a while.' I sat beside her for endless pujas, had my fortune told by the astrologer, the palmist, the parrot, and mostly listened to her. She had much to tell me about the stupidity of the servants, the difficulties in keeping insects out of her saris, the intractability of my grandmother. If the conversation ever came around to my father, she pursed her lips and turned away. If I probed, she had very little to say except that he was never around when she needed him. 'He spends as much time in that house he's given his devadasi as he does here.'

That's all I knew of my father's woman, not even that her name was Ratna, but what I gathered was that the devadasi could command attention denied to the wife. Appa had installed her conveniently in a pretty bungalow in between our house and the village, and it was her company he sought most frequently. Ratna never came to the house, unlike Nagaveni, who'd been a participant at various ceremonies when I was a child, before I knew who or what she was. She still came sometimes, and Amma treated her with more than deference, something akin to fear. Nagaveni knotted the mangala sutra at the time of weddings for the ladies in our extended family, and decorated their hair with flowers in elaborate and stylish ways, oversaw the cooking of delicious mutton dishes whenever we had a craving and folded specially flavoured paan, which caused the ladies to laugh uproariously over the mildest joke. She kept them guffawing and snorting like donkeys with her repertoire of bawdy songs.

In my schooldays, there had been a boy from a devadasi household, sent there by his wealthy father who had no sons by his legitimate wife. 'What's your father's name again?' we'd ask, pretending innocence, and then when he replied, we'd say, 'But how do you know, since your mother's a whore?'

And another boy much gossiped about in our school was just the opposite. His father had settled all his goods and property on his legal wife and children, of whom this boy was one. Having divested himself of everything he owned, he'd set up house with his devadasi in Triplicane. He worked as a lawyer and lived with the lady on a quiet street, with no one in the neighbourhood being any the wiser. But why would a man leave his family for a devadasi? It seemed a bad bargain, taking half when he could have kept the whole.

These matters were not the sort of thing I could discuss with my father. Instead, we talked about his plans for the lands in our jurisdiction, what crops he would plant, what breeds of bulls and cows he would buy, which he would keep for stud and which he would train for jallikattu, what building projects he would undertake and what equipment required repair. He did not value my opinion or place much faith in any modern ideas I had, for irrigation, say, or bringing electricity to the estate. 'First look around and take stock before coming up with crazy schemes.'

The only person with whom I conversed in a grown-up, amusing way was my grandmother. Sometimes she was in so much pain that all I could do was sit in the darkened room and let her cling to my hand, but at other times we would talk and talk for hours. She wanted to know all about England and was ever-ready to be amazed or aghast, whatever mood the stories of my adventures there demanded. I could tell her what I wouldn't dare even hint at to my mother or father. And once she fell asleep, no one missed me when I saddled my mare and rode off. Sometimes I'd take a gun and the hunting dog and a guide, but more often I'd ride out on my own.

It occurred to me that the girl – Ratna, Kanaka, Priya or Kamini, I tried out one name after another to see which one best fit – must live a jutka ride away from my cousin's village, and if I rode my horse around within that twenty-mile radius, I might come across her. It was a hopeless enterprise. A young man can't just ride into a village and hang around peering intently at every girl who goes by. People, especially villagers, don't take kindly to that sort of treatment of their womenfolk.

Anyway, it turned out that I was looking too far from home. One day, after I'd crossed the river by the bridge and hunted all day, I was leading the horse along an embankment looking for a place to let her walk down to the water to drink, while the guide waited by the road with the partridge and ducks I'd shot. That's when I saw her. I knew immediately even from that distance, glimpsed between the trunks of trees, that it was the girl from the car. It was something about the way she carried herself, the graceful tilt of her head, the curve of her neck. I had to get rid of the guide, who would surely gossip, so I sent him home with the birds, telling him to get them cleaned and cooked while I went a little further and rode home by the ridge. When he was out of sight I tethered Begum in the shade where there was long grass for her to chew, and climbed down to the water's edge. The girl was unplaiting her long braid, standing thigh-deep in water turned molten copper by the rays of the late afternoon sun. When I was almost directly opposite her across the wide expanse of the river, she saw me. I gestured that I would swim across, and she gestured no, but I took off my shirt and boots and dived in. I was showing off, I admit it. When in the deepest part, where the current was surprisingly strong, I struggled a bit, she waded in deeper herself, as if to offer me some assistance. I didn't need it, but I grabbed the hand she stretched out and let her pull me to a standing position beside her.

'It's you again,' she said. 'First a motor, now swimming. Next I expect to see you fly through the air.' Well, something like that. She teased me, which is very pleasant when a pretty girl does it, and she smiled, showing that dimple for just a moment before becoming serious. 'You mustn't be seen here. This is where the women bathe. Men must bathe further upstream. There will be a lot of bad talk if anyone catches sight of you.'

'I didn't risk my life to be sent away so quickly. I need to catch my breath. How do I ever get to talk to you? I won't go till you tell me your name and where and when we can meet again.'

'Greedy boy. That's three questions. I'll answer only one, whichever you choose.'

'That's easy. Where? I can wait there all day, and find out your name then.'

She turned to a small girl sitting on the riverbank, her back to us, so silent and still I hadn't noticed her till now. 'Durga, don't you think we should go to gather tamarind tomorrow, under the big tree beside the fallow field waiting to be planted with millet?'

I took the hint, and arrived at the tree early. I gathered up the pods while I waited, so when she came we would waste no time on that. She came running from the direction of the village along the footpath between fields, and the little silent girl ran behind her. She threw herself down beside me, saying, 'You're here. I knew you would be.' When the little girl reached us, she sat down facing away from us and stared intently at the ground in front of her without saying a word. 'Durga won't stay with anyone else, so she'll always come with me. But don't worry. She doesn't talk, so she can't tell anyone about our meeting.'

I said, 'I don't mind. Now will you tell me your name?'

'First I want to know what you guessed.'

'I tried to figure it out by logical inference. You're not hard and impenetrable like a jewel, so Ratna would never suit you, and though your skin is certainly golden, it would be unfair to your eyes and your lips and your many other attractive qualities to single that one out. So you must be Kamini or Priya. Kamini, yes, you are, but only a lover's lips should say so. But a name requires that all can use it. So I decided that you must be Priya. You are that too, and only a fool would deny it, as far as I'm concerned. Am I right?'

'But a baby is given a name for all kinds of reasons, what constellation is rising, what planet is orbiting, what number the letters make when added, don't you know that?'

'So your name isn't Priya?'

'Even if my name were not, I'd have to change it immediately so as not to offend your logic. So Priya I am. What's your name?'

'No, no, not so fast. I'm not giving my name away just like that after I had to work so hard to get yours.'

'Do I have to guess from all the names in the land? That's not fair.'

'I agree, we must play fair. So here's a riddle. Guess it right and you'll know who I'm named after:

"Like storm clouds gathering he arrives,
stealing kisses, seducing wives."'

She clapped her hands. 'Very good, I like that. It's too easy though. If only you'd let your dark curls grow, you'd look just like a Krishna.'

So I promised not to let the barber touch my hair. What could be the harm? We were both lying, though I didn't know it then. My reason was innocent, simply that I wanted to say yes to her, instead of no, that's all. I didn't learn her real name until the very end, when it was too late. She will always be Priya to me. When I found out that she had lied, I convinced myself that she was not innocent, not giving her the benefit of the doubt as I gave myself. But if she had knowingly lied to me, she must have known all along that I was lying too.

It was difficult to find times and places where we could meet unseen and unremarked. The next time it was to pick the leaves of a plant that grew at the edge of the jungle, which her mother used to make kajal, and the time after that to find a guava tree growing wild. She was not as carefully watched as girls of my own caste, but I did not inquire deeply into why that was.

Whatever formality existed between us dissolved and we moved quickly into using the intimate form of address. Our conversations were as easy as the talk between old friends. She was curious about England, so I told her about the long boat ride to get there, and the long boat ride back, the food we ate, and how we ate it with knives and forks, and the books I read, and what went on in the dorms. I could tell her anything, even about my previous encounters with women. She wasn't experienced, but she was wise to the ways of men. I didn't realize it at the time, but of course she had seen the hide-and-seek between men and women from childhood, so she was clear-eyed while I still deluded myself. I didn't know we were playing her game, and we'd play by her rules.

When she confronted me over my real name and who I was, I had no idea why it was so distressing to her. 'Why did you lie to me? It would make my life so much easier if you were indeed a Krishna, but I wish you'd told me the truth.'

'I wanted to have the name you preferred. Is it something to do with Vaishnavites and Shaivites, because all that means nothing to me. I don't believe in gods or all the silly things they want us to do.'

'Is that really so? Then . . .' and that might have been the moment she thought of telling me that she too had lied, and why. It would have been a complicated conversation requiring convoluted explanations, I know that now. She'd have to tell me unpleasant truths about my own father. Maybe that's why instead she said, 'Oh, never mind, it's not important. Come, I want to show you a place.' On this day, she'd asked me to meet her at the river, and I'd made my way along the bank, staying hidden behind the thick growth of shrubs and creepers until I saw her. She checked that no one else was in the vicinity, and as always with her sister following faithfully behind, led me along the path that went directly from the river to the village. We hadn't gone far when she left the path and headed into the undergrowth, pushing aside branches and climbing over creepers and thorny weeds. Very soon, we were completely hidden from view of the path. She continued making her way through the leaves and the closely growing trees and fallen branches, with her sister and me following, until we came to a clearing, and the old, broken stone steps of a disused tank.

'In the olden days, this tank used to fill with water from an underground spring. They say that once an elephant in rut knocked a sandalwood tree over into the tank, and the water carried the fragrance and deposited it on all who bathed there. But then the spring dried up. And as you can see there is no sandalwood tree, though someone might have cut it and carried it away. When we were small children, there used to be a track that carts used to haul away the rich silt of the tank floor. We'd follow it here and play at the bottom of these steps, where no grown-up could find us. But even we haven't come here for many years. I can reach this place by a path leading from the back gate of the temple garden, or from the river, the way we came. You must find your way here from the main road along the old cart track, without entering the village, for someone would be sure to pass remarks if you were noticed anywhere in the vicinity.'

I spent the next several days surveying the area – looking for teak trees we could cut and sell, I said, and carefully marked a narrow path to get to the tank directly from the main road. And from that day forward, that is where we met. The sister sat at the edge, and Priya and I climbed down the tumbled, disordered steps to the sandy bottom of the tank. It wasn't long before I lay with my head in her lap as we talked, and not long after that I pulled her down beside me. She came willingly into my embrace. I was the one who maintained a modicum of decorum. I didn't want her feelings for me to be her undoing. I still didn't fully understand exactly who or what she was, but this much I could tell: she saw that I wanted her, and she didn't mind, not in the least. I was the one who tried to be gentle, barely touching my lips to hers, whereas she took my lower lip between her white teeth and didn't let go, she scratched me with her fingernails, she pressed my head to her breast so that I could not but take the nipple and suck, to her great delight. I tried to be tender and slow, but she was fierce and not at all shy. She knew better than me how precious was the little time we had.

She was a virgin, but not virginal, both innocent and knowing. I was the first, the red spot on the yellow silk of her skirt was proof of that, but she behaved otherwise, already biting, scratching, pushing up against me. She seemed to know what she was doing when she shifted her weight and turned us so that she was on top. But how did she know? I say she didn't learn but knew it like the fish leaping out of the water knows what it wants from the air and the glinting sunlight.

Isn't it strange that we have one code of conduct for our mothers and sisters and wives, and quite another standard for the other kind of women? Not only in India, even in London and Paris there were the women I met in parlours and tea rooms and in the ballrooms of my wealthy British classmates, with whom I could chat and carry on polite and slightly flirtatious conversations, while the women I met in their own rooms needed no words. They read my mind, seeing my innermost thoughts and responding freely to my desires.

The next day I told my grandmother. I had to tell someone, and the words tumbled forth without forethought. Grandmother wasn't shocked or surprised. She said, 'The girl must be a devadasi from Nagaveni's household. Look and see if she has been branded with the mark of a trident on her arm. Of course, you can enjoy her, it is your right. Next time you see her you must take her a gift. No woman of her kind can give away kisses for free. When you are ready, go to Nagaveni with your offer, and terms will be discussed.' She made me close and lock the door to her room, and then pull out a tin trunk from under her bed. She wore a key on a ribbon around her neck, this she gave me to open the lock on the trunk. 'Take out everything that is underneath the saris.' I did as I was told, and unwrapped bracelets, anklets, chains, hair ornaments and many other kinds of jewellery.

I chose a gold chain from everything my grandmother had, with each link flattened and shaped like a grain of rice, and with a heart-shaped clasp. But when I gave it to Priya the next time we met, it was as if I had slapped her. In that instant I realized that I'd made a terrible mistake. My grandmother may have been right, that Priya was a girl from Nagaveni's household, but she was wrong to think a thing of value can be exchanged for what has no price. I had tried to pay for a gift that had been given freely, out of love. Priya poured the gold chain back into my hand slowly, link by link. 'It is good, about five sovereigns. Nagaveni will be pleased. She is the one with whom you can make the arrangements.' She got up to go. I knelt at her feet and held her, my arms wrapped around her hips and my face pressed into the sweet, soft skin at her waist. 'Throw the chain away, there should be no chains binding us. Don't be angry, dearest, forgive me.' And with tears and kisses we gave ourselves to each other again. That rivulet of gold lay forgotten on the smooth stone. But when she got up again and straightened her dhavani, she herself picked it up and said, 'I'll wear it underneath my skirt, where no one will see it except you.' And it circled her waist, riding just above her slender hips.

But my grandmother persisted in giving me jewels of every kind to give Priya. 'Those dancing girls, they know all the wiles. Convince a man of your love by refusing the first small gift in order to claim a greater prize later on. You must make sure that the second is even more magnificent.' 'But she has no brand on her arm.' 'You're lucky, then. You've claimed her even before her dedication ceremony, so you can be sure you're the first.' She was adamant that this is how our relationship should proceed. I gave Priya earrings in the shape of peacocks, a radiant sun of rubies and a crescent moon of pearls for her forehead, rings with diamonds and sapphires and emeralds, one each time we met, from the trove that my grandmother had brought as her dowry when she married my grandfather. One day my grandmother said, 'This is my final gift to your devadasi.' Her fingers were hardly more than bones, but she brought them to her face and slowly twisted from her nose the diamond nose pin. 'It is most auspicious to have a devadasi as part of the family,' my grandmother said. 'Your father has Ratna, and she is pretty enough, but your dancing girl is something special. The diamond in this nose pin was given to me by my father-in-law when I came to the house as the bride of his son. Give this to her now that she is part of our family.' Priya took the jewel and marvelled at its beauty. 'Why would you tell your grandmother about me? How can I ever wear it, when I am doing everything in my power to keep this a secret? Now I have to hide this too, along with all the other gifts she has given me.'

'I had to tell someone or my heart would have burst.' At first I didn't know in what way I wanted her. It's true my initial attraction was inspired by her physical beauty, but even then it was more than that simple equation. She herself made no declarations of love nor demanded any from me. And yet I had no doubt about her feelings, because she let them show on her face. I said, 'Must you go so soon?' and she replied, 'I've been here for an hour already,' and I said, 'Can't you tell some story that will allow you to stay with me the whole day?' and she said, 'There is no kind of story like that.' There was nothing out of the ordinary in the words, but her eyes spoke. When she looked at me, my insignificance was wiped away. How many kisses were our last? Never less than seven.

Sometimes without warning, the little girl, usually so silent I completely forgot her presence, would start to sing. The words of the songs came out of the child's mouth fragmented in such a way that the sound didn't immediately give up its meaning. The sense would strike me only a beat or two later, the intimate words of a woman in the throes of passion to her lover: 'If you get so tired from making love just once . . .' or 'When you make love to her, shouldn't I turn away . . .' But other times the song she sang seemed to contain a warning: 'In those days, he lit the lamp while it was still bright, so there was no moment when he couldn't see my face, but now . . .' I'd never heard these songs before, and I listened, struck by the incongruity of the strange child's pure, young voice singing such explicit lyrics. But the songs exerted a stronger power over Priya, pulling her out of my arms into some other mood in which I had no part.

This gives the impression that we were together many times, but that is not the case. I can count them on my fingers, and name each one. The first was more triumph than pleasure; the second, well, I still thought I knew what I was doing. The third was 'creeper around tree', the fourth, 'rice mixed with sesame'. By the fifth time, I knew I'd been deceiving myself: there was no moment when I'd been in control.

It would have been simplest to make our relationship known to the world by approaching her mother as my grandmother told me to do, but I felt uneasy about what such action entailed. I can't say why. Maybe I'd absorbed something of Priya's caution, for she'd hinted more than once that I should not do so. I knew nothing of the complications that kept her from suggesting that possibility, and though I can imagine it might have saved us much heartache, I'm not so sure. We might not have landed at love had we approached it by an easier path.

I know that I am a very different kind of man from my father. He has a wife, my mother, who is wise, kind, witty and so full of affection that she doesn't know what to do with it. She loves to talk, to turn everything that happens to her into a story, except that there is no one, when I'm not around, who cares to listen. My father doesn't know her, not even as well as I do. If they say a few words to each other in passing, it is over mundane details about the household, that the rice storage box has been chewed by rats, or that the man must be called to refluff the cotton in the mattresses. He doesn't know his own wife, not her secrets, her desires, her anger and hurt, or her pleasures for that matter. He isn't a bad husband, he gives her dominion over the house, he's proud of the jewels he bestows on her, but she wants more than jewels from him, and what she wants, he doesn't have to give. Now that even I am grown, there is no one who clings to her. So she's embraced god as if he were her lover. She dreams of the god, sings songs to the god, but the god is made of stone and doesn't respond.

I didn't want a marriage like that. I expected that

sometime soon, a young girl would be given into my hands as my bride, and I planned to bring her up to be my partner and my companion. I would devote myself to my wife, so that I would have a friend beside me for my whole life. When that time came, I would put Priya aside. By doing so, I would do no wrong, as neither her reputation nor her prospects would be harmed. Those were my intentions, and in themselves, not dishonourable I thought. My father's many affairs of that kind came to mind, and it occurred to me that much as I hated his habits, I was going to follow them anyway. But then it came on like a kind of illness, a fever, where it hurt to be so long separated from Priya.

She said, 'All our padams are about love at night, and it is the dawn that separates lovers. But for us, it's the opposite. While everyone else is asleep in the afternoon heat, we're together, and it is the sun low in the sky that forces us apart.' She'd already raised herself to her knees beside me and with her two slender arms above her head was gathering up and knotting her magnificent hair. Her small breasts, the nipples like tightly curled clove blossoms, the column of her neck, her winged shoulders, and below, her tiny waist that my two hands could almost encircle, the navel with a line of down leading to that triangle, everything before my eyes was so precious to me that the thought of not being with her weighed like a stone. I said, 'We must get married.

I cannot just have you in secret. I want to be with you all day and all night.'

Times were changing. The raja of Puddukottai had married an Australian woman, and the raja of Ramnad had taken a devadasi as his second wife. The Self-Respect movement was promoting marriages of this kind, where a man and a woman didn't consider caste and status but met each other and joined as equals, without priests, without any ritual except their own loving words. So our coming together should amaze no one. I was taken by surprise when she wouldn't countenance it. She had a poor idea of marriage. A wife, in her estimation, was no better than a slave and she refused me outright. 'Don't you know the proverb "A loving girl is no good for marriage; a girl for marriage is no good for loving?"' and she sang that song in Nattakuravanji, 'A bride's life in a lord's family / I wouldn't wish it on my enemy / Some days pass in obeying one's elders / some days pass in meaningless courtesies / some days pass without pleasure from your husband / while every day youth's bloom is fading / with passion as elusive as moonlight in the jungle.'

Her beauty and accomplishments, quick wit and playful, passionate nature, natural and appropriate for a devadasi, were not the qualities the world would judge as suitable for a wife, but I was willing to overlook the discrepancy in our relative status out of love for her. She was so proud of her lineage that joining my family was no adequate substitute for giving up her own, which went back so many generations that Indra and celestial damsels came into that history. I told her, 'If you don't marry me, my mother is going to make sure that someone does.' She didn't seem to mind, and said with a smile, 'Your mother will bless me for having refused, so that she can have the kind of daughter-in-law she's been yearning for. I'm not trained in household tasks. All I know is how to sing and dance.'

Moreover, she thought I was deluded about the very nature of love to take so seriously my own feelings. 'If stolen love turns into married love, then it is full of strife and jealousy.' She brought up that tired old metaphor, of the man like the bee drinking from flower after flower. But that is stupid, I said to her, a man is not like a flying insect. 'Nor is a moonbeam like an arrow, and yet it pierces me when I lie awake at night and think of you.' That's how I lost every argument, surrendering to desire that seemed to overwhelm us both at the same moment and in equal measure. The difference was that she thought me naive to believe that this emotion we both shared so fully was, or could be, permanent, while I thought she was naive to believe that it hadn't found its way permanently and irrevocably into her heart. 'Are you saying your feelings for me will change?' 'All flowers,' she replied, 'drop their petals.' Yet, I felt she was wholly mine, and I feared for her, that she might not realize it until she'd forced us apart.

I put it to her bluntly: 'Don't tell me this is what you really want, to lie with one man and then another?' She rejoined, 'Imagine your dear mother, falling to her knees at your feet, begging and pleading. Are you telling me that her tears would mean nothing to you? Or do you think there is something you can say that will cause her to welcome me with lighted camphor when you take me to your home? Our lives are circumscribed. Do you rail because night follows day? Why must you spoil this very moment, now, here, by thinking about the future?' And letting her pallav fall, she'd begin to untie the knot of her bodice.

The real sticking point between us though was that she refused to even try to imagine a life in which she did not dance. At the same time, she perfectly recognized that no wife of mine could show herself in places where any man could stare at her. A roomful of men, looking at my wife, lusting after her, watching her dance those padams and javalis, pretending to undress, becoming naked in their minds, describing lovemaking in detail – kisses, pinching of nipples, placing of legs, bites, nail marks. She's making love with Krishna, but so what? Gods want the same things that men want. Any man on the street could imagine himself within her embrace, could do to her in his head all the things she mimed Krishna doing. How could I live with that?

I wanted her, and she wanted to dance. There seemed to be no possible way to break this impasse until the maidservant brought me that note while I was sitting with my uncle. It said we'd run away to Madras and marry, exactly as I'd wanted. If Janardana's words hadn't first confused me and then filled me with a choking, visceral revulsion, I would have rejoiced at her change of heart and rushed to meet her as she'd instructed. Instead, I was overcome by nausea at her assumption that our relationship would not matter to me, since it had not mattered to my father. So she was right after all, feelings do change. With that change of heart the whole world changed. The evening sky lost its radiance. I paced back and forth in the garden and this time, when for solace I bent towards the roses, I saw they were being eaten by worms. I didn't go to her. Instead, I drank myself into a stupor, watching the fireflies flicker, impotent against the dark and silence.

After the accident, in the delirium induced by the scorpion's poison, I saw her many times, but always walking away, her long braid and the sway of her hips. I tried to run after her but the ground turned to quicksand. During the endless days of illness and separation, my feelings changed yet again. I thought, I don't care, let her be whoever she is, and I said to her in my heart, I'm ready now, I'll come to you wherever you are. But by then word of the statue in the temple reached even my ears. I guessed she'd somehow run away without my help. The golden image looks nothing like her, and anyway, I don't believe in god and his miracles. She must have had someone's help. I began to wonder, had it all been artifice? She'd never pretended to be other than what she was, but her art seemed to be like that of the magician who pretends to show you how a trick is done while the real trick is kept secret – he is picking your pocket.

Then the body was dragged out of the well, and I was in hell again; it seemed that she was the one who'd loved more deeply after all, and I, by my change of heart, had caused her such torment as only death could resolve. When the truth finally came to be known, it brought no sense of relief. How could it?

I can't help wondering at which point events could have unfolded otherwise. If Janardana had not been there when the maid brought the note, if he had not talked, if I had trusted her instead of believing what came out of his mouth, if she had trusted me and told me when she had the chance the facts of her birth, so that what Janardana said didn't come as a rude shock, if, if, if, if, if. But it's too late for blame or mourning.

Even in dreams, the world never glows as it did in the moments when I heard the rustle of her footsteps and watched as she emerged, blazing gold, through the curtain of green leaves and shifting shadows. If the nightingale still sings somewhere, I no longer hear it. The English call this sensation heartbreak, as if the thing inside is thin and brittle, cracking like sugar candy. But the sensation I feel is heaviness, of something soaked and sodden in my chest. Or maybe that's a residue of the scorpion sting. Nowadays I try to catch the thought of her before I think it, but I'm always too late, deep into some memory before I even realize it.

My mother is nagging me again about my marriage. This time I'm inclined to let her have her way. After all, it's been almost five years now. The horoscopes match and my uncle says she's not so very plain for a girl with a big dowry. The truth is, I pity any girl who becomes my wife.

Police Sub-Inspector Mir Husain Sahib

This is how the body came to be found.

At the north-eastern edge of the village, there was a house that had been locked up for several months because of some conflict between relatives. A watchman had been deputed to keep an eye on the property and make sure that one relative did not try to dispose of the property without the other one's knowledge. This full-moon night, the watchman claimed that when, for whatever reason, he looked into the well, he saw a pair of eyes staring back at him. Being thoroughly frightened, he ran to the Mariamman temple and stayed there awake and shivering, waiting for the morning light. As soon as dawn broke, he went to the village headman with the story. But when the village headman came, along with several of his relatives and friends, he saw nothing. The well was about twenty feet deep and covered with water hyacinth from months of disuse. Still, the watchman insisted that he had seen the eyes staring at him, so an agile youngster was put into a bucket and lowered into the well. The little boy saw not a face, but a bare bloated stomach.

One man was dispatched at this juncture to contact the police constable in Kumbakonam taluk, the nearest one, about 18 kilometres away. Meanwhile, several men of the toddy tapper caste, perhaps because of their climbing skills, or their reputation for ingenuity, agreed to get the body out. But then the question of their caste became an issue, as their entering the water would pollute it, and render it unusable. No one of the requisite higher castes was willing, or even able, to undertake this unpleasant task, so there was an impasse until the priest mentioned that he could perform a ritual to remove the pollution caused by the touch of the pariah caste of toddy tappers, and they were allowed to proceed. With a system of ropes and a large tarpaulin that had provided some shade in front of the dry goods store, they were able to accomplish the task. By that time, quite a crowd had gathered and were on hand to see the half-naked body of the girl laid out on the bare earth. Unfortunately, this crowd included the dead girl's own mother and sisters.

They had not reported the girl missing. That in itself constitutes another story, which I will come to later.

The dead girl was a nautch girl from the Navagraha temple, by the name Kanakavalli. Two weeks prior, she had not turned up for the ritual waving of the pot lamp which was her duty and which she had performed without fail for the past ten months, in place of her older sister, Ratnavalli, whose responsibility it had been until that time.

Under harsh questioning, the watchman confessed to a more plausible sequence of events. The man was not a conscientious watchman by any means. Instead of doing his job, he'd learned to anticipate the habits of his employer, who lived in another village and came to check up on the property at fairly regular but infrequent intervals, never less than a fortnight or more than three weeks. As long as the watchman made sure to be on the premises looking alert and fearless, and the grounds were reasonably neat during the period when a visit was likely, he could indulge his propensities for drink and gambling without fear of discovery in the interim. He'd spent the time from the last visit of his employer, just before Ekadasi, at the places where local liquor was made and sold, or wherever there were cockfights or koothus. Now that the moon was nearing fullness, he'd been assiduous in catching up with neglected tasks. That is how the body in the well came so late to his notice.

He had slept at the house only infrequently, spending more time away playing cards and drinking toddy. When he set about making the place ready for inspection, the house itself was exactly as he left it, doors still locked, windows still shuttered. This well is not used now and had already been neglected for some months when the watchman arrived to take up his duties. So rather than get the well cleaned and made usable, he was in the habit of bathing at the river and carrying up a pot for his bit of washing and drinking during the day. Until now the bucket and rope had been at the side of the well, the old rope threaded through the pulley, the rusty bucket turned upside down just as the owners had left it, should he have wanted to use them. For the first time he noticed the bucket was not beside, but in the well, with the end of the rope stuck in the pulley. At first, seeing that the house had not been broken into, he purposely ignored this sign. But with the other strange happenings in the village, which I haven't yet got to, he became more and more convinced that there was something in the well. On this day, he steeled himself to check. He managed to dislodge the rope and was pulling the bucket straight up and full of water, hand over hand, when as it neared the surface it snagged on something. That is when he looked into the well, and saw not eyes, but an arm, caught on the edge of the bucket. He dropped the bucket and ran, and the rest of the story is as he told it.

Now to the story of the nautch girl and why she hadn't

been reported missing. Kanakavalli was the girl who performed the temple duties along with the priest, and she had been doing this for the last ten months. Till about two weeks ago, Kanakavalli had never been late or swerved by one hair's breadth, it seems, in preparing everything for the priest exactly as he had instructed her to the very last detail. In the month or so immediately prior to this, according to the priest, she had never actually done anything amiss, but had seemed more rushed and less meticulous in her preparations of flowers, lamp and ritual articles. Two weeks ago, at the time of the first puja in the temple, which was at 5.40 a.m., the priest came there ready to perform the ceremony, but found that no preparations had been made, nor was Kanakavalli anywhere to be seen. This was an important ritual day of Ekadasi, the first day of the new moon, so the priest was especially upset. Still, since the ritual awakening of the deity had to be performed at the auspicious time, the sanctum sanctorum was opened for the puja without her. When the priest lit the lamps, lo and behold, there was a little golden statue of the girl – Kanaka means 'gold' – in the characteristic pose of temple attendant.

Therefore, this was taken as a proven fact – the girl had turned herself into a statue! So why look for her at all? Immediately, word spread in the surrounding villages, and by the evening, the temple was full of devotees wanting to witness the miracle. The money that came into the temple donation box in the last two days was more than in the whole of last year, and the priest, and the girl's mother, all had a very good reason to look no further into her disappearance than this 'miracle'. But now, with the discovery of the girl's body, it seems to be not so miraculous after all.

Could the girl have jumped into the well? This was highly unlikely. The body was found half-naked. There was no conceivable way for a young girl to have made her way from her house, which is near the temple, through the streets in that condition. On the other hand, if she had stripped just before jumping in, and why she might have done so would still remain to be explained, her blouse and upper cloth should be nearby, but so far no such garments have been found. In any case, our forensic examination will answer the question conclusively.

The Priest

Here in the western corner is the Kalyana Mandapa. The plinth is low, with rounded mouldings interrupted in the cardinal directions and at the corners by niches that contain the images of the gods for the four chief and four subsidiary directions, the world protectors. See, here facing south is Yama, riding on a water buffalo. Karma, which once created must be endured, for it does not dissipate, even in tens of millions of ages, is the noose he carries. His number is nine.

Yama's own death was the first death. He led the way, marked for us the path to his realm. Agni, fire, is his priest, burning up the dead like logs, and behind him are his five attendants: Time, Fever, Disease, Anger and Jealousy. Is it one of these servants of Yama who disturbs you and brings you to seek my advice? You are not alone. Who alive has not been touched by Death or the servants of Death? No one.

Living is just the word we use for dying. From the moment we're born, the god is ever inching closer. Do you feel him nearing as I do? We must be ready to welcome him when he comes. If you make offerings during your lifetime you need not fear him later on. Lay a flower here at the base, that Death may treat you gently, as that is all you can ask. He shows his smile only to the righteous, and to the wicked he metes out justice with sternness but without losing his calm. He can't be fooled by lies told with conviction, for truth alone reflects the sparkle of his diamond gaze.

Let us continue up these steps, with the fierce lion faces of yaalis, teeth bared, long trunk like an elephant's, on either side of the banister. Look at the intricately carved outer pillars, each with a skilful rider pulling hard on the bejewelled reins of his caparisoned horse so that it rears up, front hooves about to fall on the enemy cowering underneath his shield, useless as it is to save him. This is it, the moment before death suspended in the stone so that we can look on this precise instant and marvel. On the central pillars, the sculptor has carved the simulacra of life. The figures seem to emerge almost fully from the stone so that you can see them, front, back and sides. Facing inside are women, each in her own graceful posture. Even the hairstyles are different – one wears a long braid, another has cascading ringlets, another a high, tight side bun and one a low, loose knot at the nape of her neck. One carries a fly whisk, another sandalwood paste in a silver bowl, another flowers, another rose water ready to sprinkle. On the opposite side, facing outward are fierce yaalis standing up on their strong back legs, showing their slender-waisted leonine bodies, mouths open to reveal pointed teeth. On that side, arms curve, on this side, snouts curve. On that side, breasts bulge, on this side, fierce eyes bulge. Here, put your hand inside this yaali's mouth. It is said the man who carved this dreamt one night of a certain special tool but could not imagine how it was to be used. Still, he went to the trouble of explaining his idea to the iron worker, who somehow or the other made it for him from his description. Without knowing what he was trying to do, he set to work with his unique chisel. This, then, is what he was able to carve. Can you feel how the ball in the beast's mouth turns freely in the cage of his teeth? Somehow the tool was lost, and no one else has been able to dream it into existence, so there is only one such pillar in the whole temple.

There are other wonders here. These pillars when struck each play a pure note. Listen! This one is *sa*, this one *ma*, this one *pa*. When musicians tune their instruments to the right pitch, the stone itself resonates. This corner is the place for telling secrets. If I go here, all the way across from you and you whisper into the stone, I can hear what you say.

Few remember to look up, but the sculptors didn't skimp

on their work on the ceiling. In the old days, when I used to be the priest of this temple, once all the worshippers left and I had the temple to myself, I would lie on my back and stare into the stone until its geometry filled my vision. It is as beautiful as any sky full of clouds and birds. The centre is a lotus of a thousand petals, blooming like the noonday sun. Around that are eight smaller lotuses on which the gods of the eight directions stand, and around that, the nine planets, and around that the twelve astrological signs. Now I must enter the temple in secret after everyone has gone when it is too dark to see anything. I stare up into the darkness, and trace each contour and groove with my mind. If I look long enough, the figures move a little, as if the petals are ruffled by a breeze. The eyes of the gods open and close, as if they are looking down at me while I look up at them. They take on colours they were once painted in, turquoise and orange and pink.

The sage Kashyapa had two wives, though why, you might ask, when he had no use for even one. You may think I'm repeating a story you already know, but even if the names and the incidents are the same, this is different, the one that my father told me, and his father told him, each of them holding in their hands the palm leaves on which it is written. The pages are too fragile to open and read, a promissory note for veracity that cannot be redeemed. I don't know why the stories are so similar and yet vary on both minor details and crucial points; I can only repeat what my father said as he laid the palm leaves, dry and folded like closed eyelids so they rested almost weightless in my small, outstretched hands. He said 'two wives' and to match the words, he held up two fingers, one of each hand, as if pointing to one wife, here, and one wife, there, 'and two eggs' as each hand then turned and curved to show the weight and shape and value of the gift it held. Having given each wife her gift, Kashyapa left them and went about his own business of praying, doing penance and making the gods afraid of his immense spiritual power. Each wife took her precious egg, kept it warm and watched over it to ensure that nothing disturbed its unbroken sleep, while its mystery pervaded all her imaginings. Then one day after much waiting and hoping and praying, when the wives had begun to wonder if this was all a joke played on them by their temperamental husband, at an auspicious moment, one egg cracked open and the shell fell away to reveal a bird, tiny at first, but growing by the minute.

My father then sang a verse in praise of the bird thus born, for that was Garuda, who carries the god Vishnu on his back: *'netramgayatramuce trivrut iti ca siro namadheyam yajumshi chandamsi angani dhishnyatmabhi: ajani aphai: vigraho vamadevyami yasya stomatmana: asau brhat itara garut tadrsaamnata puccha: svacchandyamna:*

prasutamsrutisata Sikhara abhishtutatmaa garutman' (Garuda Panchassat, Verse 3).

(His eyes, the Gayathri mantra, his head, the Trivrth mantra, his name, the Yajurveda, his limbs, the study of Vedic meters, his hooves, the altar called dhishnya, his body, wings and tail other songs and mantras, his very self, hymns of praise. May Garuda thus extolled show us the way to freedom.)

Father wanted Garuda's protection for me from the poison of snakes, having foreseen perhaps in my horoscope such a problem as I am now victim to, for they say this disease is caused by the curse of a snake. But don't think just because you see me in this condition that the mantra doesn't work. It has its own efficacy. As I repeat it now, it protects you, not only from snakes, but from the fear you harbour of what lies ahead, the future like a python with its unhinged jaws open and ready to swallow you.

Just try to imagine the other wife's feelings. Her rival's egg had hatched and by the time the mother had finished singing her first lullaby, the bird was as big as a chariot, while her own egg remained as still and silent as ever. She continued to sit, watching, waiting, waiting, watching, while day after day nothing happened. On the outside the egg remained enigmatic, revealing nothing. A little but persistent voice began nagging inside her head. 'What if your little bird can't get out? Perhaps it is suffocating inside this too-thick shell. Maybe it needs a little help.' At first she silenced that voice with her own mantra, 'Wait, wait, wait, wait,' but instead of fading away, the voice returned louder and more vehemently, making her fear for the well-being of whatever it was that grew inside her own egg. 'Just make a tiny hole,' it said. 'Peek in. Make sure everything is as it should be.' Finally, after many more days and months of fruitless waiting, she gave in to the voice, and tried to make a tiny hole to look in. Alas, as anyone with any sense knows, an egg can't be cracked just a little. Inside was a baby, perfect and beautifully formed in every way on the top half, while below was only the amorphous mass of the legs, the development of which she had halted through her impatience. This half-formed child cursed his mother to be a slave for her impatience. With his strong arms and manly chest, he became the charioteer of the Sun. Every morning it is this half-being Arunan you see, in the red dawn before the sun appears.

When Surya was afflicted with severe pain he prayed and did penance to Shiva for an end to his suffering. It is said that Arunan brought him here, to this very spot, to find some relief. See the dark discoloration in the granite, shaped like a man lying on his side, legs drawn in by his agony, where his brilliance, though dimmed, still burned into the stone.

I see you are not yet ready to ask your question. That is

fine. Meanwhile, this temple deserves your full attention. There is no point in rushing. When the answer is given before it's ready, it will be half-formed, and its incompleteness will bind you.

Since you remain silent, let me tell you my story. It is the power of the priest's penance that brings the devotee into the divine presence that has entered the icon. So it is important that those who perform the temple rituals behave according to dharma. It is no use to hide our actions, for Manu says: 'The sky, the earth, the waters, the heart, the moon, the sun, the fire, Yama and the wind, the night, the two twilights, and justice know the conduct of all corporeal beings.'

From the first time Nagaveni mentioned to me what she wanted, I knew it to be wrong, though no one else would say so. It is not written in any text that what I contemplated was a sin, while kicking a cow, facing sun or moon while defecating, or sleeping with the guru's wife are specifically mentioned. Our scriptures equivocate about such actions, for even the gods are helpless when filled with desire, even for a woman who is his daughter, or another's wife, or a male in disguise. And I could tell myself that if I didn't do it, Nagaveni would find someone else. So who better, me or a man Ratna didn't even know? I could take her pretty little hand, I could touch her where I liked, I could taste her.

The small, low room had never contained anything so

bright as that girl as she shone in the light of the oil lamp. If I'd looked at her frightened face I couldn't have gone on with it, so I kept my eyes on the slope of her small breasts. But every time I lay with Ratna, lust was so mixed with shame and pity and horror at my own abasement that I earned fully the gold coin that Nagaveni gave me when Ratna missed her courses. I had known the thing was wrong, and I had done it anyway. In my deepest, most secret being I was afraid, had the opportunity come my way again, I would once more succumb to desire. And that was not the kind of man I wanted to be.

People around me said I was wise. I never raised my voice in anger, or cheated a man out of even one pie. I studied the holy books, I knew what should be done and what should not be done. If I was a good man then what a good man wanted would also be good, for how could an evil desire ever arise in the midst of my goodness? But even the gods cannot resist such temptations so what hope was there for me?

Try it yourself. Not do something you truly, deeply desire. See for how long you can resist, how much time you spend thinking of what it is you don't want to do, how it becomes the only thing you think about, obliterating all other thoughts, how the only way you can drive it from your mind is to give in.

Being the village priest is not an onerous job. It brings

money, security, prestige. My decision to leave profession, home and family was not taken lightly. I felt the cost. You may ask, 'Was there no other way to do it, without causing so much pain?' My answer is that I tried all those methods first, one ritual after another without success in assuaging the guilt that had become a constant burden. By the tenth year it was so heavy my back was breaking. The pain I would cause especially to Subbu, my young son, was a grave consideration, but you must understand that I knew pain was coming to them from my actions no matter what I did. Perhaps in some way my leaving would lessen it.

Others, great men, Buddha, Mahavira, left sleeping wives and children without saying a word, so I felt my impulse was not without precedent. But I set out not for moksha or union with Brahman, or to discover the nature of the universe or open my third eye. I wanted only to learn how not to do what I knew to be wrong, to act in opposition to what I desired.

I left the house and village and temple to wander, thinking that I could choose my own punishment. The gods had other ideas, and visited on me a punishment of their own, thus you see me in this condition. I can't tell you the exact moment this disease took hold. First a white patch on my knee that became rough and scaly, where the skin could not feel touch, that spread inexorably. A knotting of the lobes of my ears. Numbness in my hands and feet. My voice became hoarse and my breath offensive. Maha Kustha, that is what it is called. There were amulets, ointments, herbs and roots, massage with neem leaves, powdered cobra meat, charmugra oil, rubbed and swallowed, but as you can see nothing stayed the course of the disease within me. Manu says, 'Some evil-minded persons for sins committed in this life suffer a morbid change in their bodies. They bear the marks of their as yet unexpiated sins, so that an atrocious sinner is struck by Maha Kustha.' This is all that gives me hope, for I don't mind this suffering if it means I can expunge my sin in this birth.

I took up the cloak of poverty and moved from temple to temple. When my disease was not so obvious I was able to earn some money through the practice of looking into the nature of the planetary influences driving a person's misfortunes. I sat in the outer courtyards of temples telling men how to safeguard their business investments or telling women the means to cure their childlessness. Sometimes the advice I whispered into the wife's ear was, 'By any means possible, lie with your brother-in-law,' and I would give her a special mixture of herbs. The woman would be sure to say to all who cared to listen, 'My child was born after my husband drank the potion given by the Brahmin who sits in the temple,' not mentioning that the drink didn't make her man more potent, a difficult thing to achieve. Rather it succeeded by the simpler expedient of putting him into a deep sleep that allowed her to follow the other part of my instruction. Being right once or twice is all that is required to gain a reputation for always being right.

But now my only recourse is to beg, to sit as one among the row of deformed, deranged, armless, blind creatures who accept what pittance the devotee may choose to give. That thread that I've worn since my eighth year and that once marked me as a superior being lost all meaning once I began eating food given to me by anyone and sleeping between dogs and pigs. I who was a Brahmin am now a pariah.

You may be surprised to know that in one respect both conditions are similar. Both expand one's being beyond one's own skin. As a Brahmin I inhabited a larger space because of my sanctity, so that all who might pollute it – those who beat the leather drums, who work with carcasses and leather hides, who clean human waste with their bare hands – backed away at my coming, so that even their shadows didn't enter the air I breathed. Now it is the miasma floating around me that causes a person to avert their eyes, to flinch and step back when I come near and drop their coin into my misshapen hand from a great height. I'm a bad omen, where I used to be a good one, to see me as one sets out on a journey or begins an important task will bring failure, where it used to bring success. I've got used to that reaction because it is not so very different – I'm still a portent.

But at the same time the disease extended my presence in the world, it diminished me too. I started drawing away from that thin edge where I end and the world begins. I used to feel it between my feet and the road, with its small stones and its dust, between my fingers and the rough clay of the cup, between my face and the hot humid air. Now when I touch it is without sensing what I touch, whether stone or wood or skin. I end somewhere deeper inside this carapace. That's why my son, my wife, my brother-in-law walk past me but do not see the man they once knew. All they or you or anyone sees is this shell of my affliction.

I have returned here after so many years of wandering because no matter where I went I wasn't able to rid myself of my sin. The evil that I'd done could not be left behind like an upper cloth forgotten on a bench, or discarded like the banana leaf after the vadai wrapped within it has been eaten, or dropped like a five-anna coin in a beggar's bowl. It clung to me more tightly than my own skin, which as you can see has fallen away in places.

Yet here you are, come to this distant, unknown temple because you need what only I can provide. I will do my best for you. But remember this: like the two horns of a cow, just because two things occurred together, at the same time and the same place, doesn't mean that one thing caused the other.

The sense in all events is what we make of it. Even if

eventually the cause will always give rise to its effect, we don't remember evil acts done in other lives, so when in this life the consequences of those actions play out, they seem arbitrary, meaningless. Without a perfect understanding of karma all we can do in the present is minimize the harm we do. My advice has always been about that.

Let me give you an example. When Vallabendran was younger, he was much given to drinking and gambling, causing his father and mother a great deal of distress and worry. The raja asked me to look at his horoscope and ascertain if there was some dosha or ill-placed star which could be counteracted with amulets or spells or temple rituals.

I called Vallabendran to me and showed him his chart. I said, 'This configuration, where Mercury, the god of luck in gambling, and Venus, the goddess of intoxication, are directly in confrontation – they cancel each other out. If you are intoxicated while you gamble, you will not win, there is no chance with such a positioning of the planets. You should be sober when you throw the dice.' Till that moment, the two had always gone together for Vallabendran: when he drank, he gambled, and when he gambled, he drank. And I had not said to him 'don't drink' or 'don't gamble'. All I told him was that his luck would desert him if he drank. Perhaps because we are both the same age, he listened to me. Soon after, when he won a little, not being made insensible by drink, he stopped throwing down the cards so that he could lift the glass to his lips. Money started collecting in his purse and stayed there. And consider, is it that the two planets were in opposition? Would anyone else have seen what I brought to his attention? There is a mountain of detail in anyone's chart and often what I see, only I can see. From such predictions did my reputation as an astrologer grow.

It was when I saw the baby for the first time that my heart wrenched and I fully understood what I'd done. She gazed up at me with big, serious eyes as if she knew me for who I was to her and reached out and held on to one finger, bringing it to her mouth and chewing on it with much cooing and gurgling. After that, I struggled to change the rhythm of the dance I had set into motion. I couldn't bear the thought that kept coming to me as she grew into such a pretty, clever child, that some man would use her as I had used her mother to produce her. Some man she looked on kindly, someone she called 'Older Brother' or 'Uncle' or even 'Father', would hold her down as she cried and begged him to let her go, and do to her exactly what I had done to Ratna.

I'd been given gold in exchange for my seed that had made this child, but I couldn't bring myself to spend it. My wife would have believed any story I told to explain its existence and she would have used it wisely to ease the burden of keeping the household running, but I didn't want to use that precious coin for some mundane transaction. I hid it away among my palm leaf manuscripts and tried to forget that it was there. When I left, I carried it with me thinking I would drop it into the offering box of some temple with a greater and more powerful and benevolent god, one who would save me for this price.

Now do you understand why I had to make my way from one pilgrimage site to another? But even that was not enough. No god will, but perhaps this disease will wipe out the sin in this lifetime.

Nagaveni

How do you keep a man wanting more? You make him wait. You say no and then yes, yes and then no. Love is a science like any other, and we have studied long to discover the rules; we practise them, we make them perfect. What do the ancient sages say is the highest attainment? Moksha. And what do they say moksha is like? Like making love. And that is freely available to us, without putting our bodies through any tribulations. What I say is, if we are going to make love, then why not put the effort into it that our yogis put into attaining moksha? If we strive to find out what it is that gives our man pleasure, what it is that gives us pleasure, then I ask you, where is the need for moksha at all?

This is what I know from my relationships with men: if you give them what they want, when they want it, they are not happy. Make them wait. Say, 'You didn't come yesterday, when I waited and waited for you, why come now? I'm no longer in the mood.' Or 'Is your wife having her period? And you expect me to pick up the slack? No way!'

Or 'What is this? You finally visit me after a long time, and expect to get right down to business? No, wait. First I must dress myself to receive you. I haven't even put flowers in my hair. Sit there, far away. Don't grab me like that.'

Or 'Let me prepare the bed. You are going to be here for two or three hours at least. Last time you left without satisfying me fully. This time I'm not going to let you go so easily.'

You observe his mood. If he comes in the mood for sex, then you can afford to tease him a little, cast doubts on his manhood, his ability to please you. If he seems tired, or you sense that he has come out of a feeling of obligation, then don't even mention his absence, and don't belabour the allusions to intercourse. Let him relax. Play cards with him, feed him, ply him with drink. Massage his head or his feet, sing to him.

If you are not sure about his erection, go slow, very slow, for failure must never happen. He must never come to doubt his own prowess, for that only brings about the very thing he fears. When a man's erection is not a sure thing, he becomes anxious, he gets depressed. So it is paramount that if you see he may not manage it you call things off before he becomes aware of his own shortcoming. Say, 'I am not in the mood for that, let's do this.' Or this is the moment to put another woman in his way. For, have you not observed how the cock will not mount the hens in his henhouse, but throw in a new hen, and he will immediately rise to the occasion? Let your maid – make sure she is a pretty one! – come in with her sari all tucked up to show her round calves, and ask her to massage his head, while you attend to something in the kitchen. And if you come back to find that he has staked his claim to her, don't even pretend to be angry. Laugh, and say, 'My loss is her gain. Couldn't you have waited a few more minutes?' Then tease him, and tease her too, so that he knows in your house he is always sure of satisfaction one way or the other.

Of course, we know all the techniques. We learn to satisfy our men with our mouths from the hijras – they are the experts in that form of lovemaking. But what they can do with their mouths, we can do with our vaginas. We train those muscles too, not just the ones we use for dance.

We are descended from the apsaras, who rose like butter during the churning of the ocean. They were so beautiful that neither gods nor demons dared to take them as wives. It was agreed that they would be common to all, free to love whom they chose.

And don't you know that the poet Kalamekar acquired

the gift of singing verses in sweet Tamil by taking the half-chewed paan from a devadasi's mouth?

We are not low-class women who wear garish make-up, are indecent and aggressive, who use bad words, who consort with poor and low-caste men, who service the police to keep them in line and who spread disease. That is not our kind of work. We instead speak politely with proper grammar and a soft voice, do our work for the deity in the temple, alongside practising the arts of our lineage, much appreciated by Brahmins and elite noblemen.

The padams and javalis we sing and dance create the mood, get the man thinking on the right lines. Before he ever sees our breasts, we get him imagining how they look and feel. We describe the shape, the size, the weight of them. Then only does he fall upon our fruits, sucking and squeezing to his heart's content.

Look at this hair, still black, not a trace of grey. Before I wash it, I rub it with a paste made of henna root to give a bluish sheen to the black. I wash it with soapnut ground with dried lime rinds. To dry it, I lie with it spread like a peacock's tail on a woven bamboo basket in which is kept a brazier burning frankincense, so each strand is imbued with the fragrance. When a man unravels my braid, he is intoxicated. Such is the trouble I take to ever be in an alluring state, ever-ready for my lover's attention, on whichever part of my body it happens to fall.

Now which wife will have the time for all this? She has to think of the children, the parents-in-law, and all their demands: the meals, the pujas, the festival days, the purchase of provisions. If her husband comes at an inopportune moment, she says, 'Not now, can't you think of more important things?' Even the man will be afraid, he'll think, 'I already have six children, what if I get one more?,' and he himself will lose his erection and slink off.

But the ultimate truth we know about love is that it is beyond our command. It comes, it goes. We accept that. If after some time he no longer feels his heart leap, his blood rise at the sight of us, well, then, so be it. He may leave us at any time, and so may we leave. I do not have to care for my lover in his old age, wash his limbs covered with boils, or kiss his gummy mouth when his teeth fall out, as Manu says a good wife must do.

We keep passion alive as long as we can, but when it dies, we don't lament over it. We know that he will try to find it again with someone else, and good luck to him. But that is why we're careful to accumulate gifts. When he is in love, he will be generous. When he moves on, the new dasi will demand, and he will forget us. So we know what we have to get and when, and if we forget we have our mothers to remind us. And growing old, we teach our daughters all the tricks we've learned.

When Vallabendran first came to me, he did not leave my bed for three days, not even to eat. I was sore inside and out. All the places he bit me! He was a young man then. Oh well, I don't complain. I'm the one who told him, 'Now it is time for you to get married,' and I'm the one who saw to it that he treated the girl well. I sent one of my own maids to work in her household and keep me informed of the situation there. Every month, when the wife's red river began its flow, the maid came with a polished copper pot filled with water and hibiscus flowers, which she would pour over his feet. 'Go home,' I'd say, 'and treat your wife with every courtesy for these three days when you cannot touch her. Then on the fourth day, she will let you do as you like, without any jealousy. For jealousy will heat the body and harm the embryo if she conceives.' I took care of all such matters.

I never loved him; when you love it is harder to practise wiles and play the games that retaining his interest requires. This is why we don't mind if the girl has a man she is in love with from our own community. She can get her satisfaction from him, and the patron need never know. And even if he suspects and thinks to himself, 'Why is that dark-skinned mridangam player hanging around?,' it is like a jackal trying to nip a piece of the tiger's kill – he need only once in a while roar and show his teeth for the man to take himself off. He too knows where the rice comes from that feeds us all and he would be very careful to do nothing that jeopardizes that.

And if once in a while a girl is so beautiful, and a patron so besotted that he regularizes his union with her – well, it happens – it doesn't please us. It is a loss to our community.

But the times are changing. Devadasis are getting a bad reputation, and the laws are becoming strict – a girl is not to be dedicated until she is sixteen. Sixteen! Which man will believe a girl of sixteen is still a virgin, and pay the price for that? This new India will not have devadasis in it, it seems. If that is so, then what can I say. Except this: men's natures will not change so suddenly, or women's either. Or love itself, which not everyone has the art and skill and science to nurture. It is not as if men will suddenly be content to make love once in a while to the woman whose flaccid breasts suckled all his children. The world will not change that much, whatever you say. I for one have no desire for domesticity. Look at me, old and fat, and yet Dorai sleeps in my bed and not with his wife half my age. What he finds between my thighs is sweet and juicy still.

We sat together on the mat in the front room. I could see by the tiny beads of sweat on his upper lip how our talk had heated him. I picked up the palmyra leaf fan and waved it gently over him. I called out to Ratna, 'Bring Pasupati anna a glass of buttermilk.' Yes, a Brahmin may drink in a devadasi's household. The girl came in from the kitchen with the tumbler and handed it to him. He took it from her without meeting her eyes, and tilted his head back and poured it into his mouth without the rim touching his lips.

If you know that a man cannot do something, and yet you go to him to get the thing done, then people would say you really don't know how to go about things, wouldn't they? I knew his answer when I made my proposition to him. I said, 'The girl is too heated, she needs this to cool her down,' and the priest said, 'I will have to think about it,' but I could tell that in his heart he had already said yes. Now he would go and all alone at night he would let his thoughts range over the act he was about to do. He would convince himself that what he desired was also right, and marshal all his priestly moral arguments to dignify the decision he'd already arrived at through the coursing of his blood.

Had he ever considered such a thing before I proposed it? Of course he had! He had watched the girl grow, had observed her development, her feminine attributes, her sidelong glances, her shy smiles. He could tell himself there was no wrong in this because she was there to serve exactly that purpose, to attract the lustful glances of men. He could see that Ratna was no innocent. She knew very well that some men who came to the temple came only to see her.

'I could take her, take her pretty little hand, I could touch her skin, where I like, I could taste her.' Those were the thoughts I could see on his face.

And if he said no, wouldn't I be disappointed? I'd have to find someone else to do the job. He knew that. I had only to settle his worries.

'Your wife would never come to know. She is away for her confinement,' I said. 'And for all you know, she might encourage you, for the sake of the gold coin I offer as compensation for your seed. Brhadambal knows a bargain.' Of course, he knew perfectly well that his plain, shy wife, Brhadambal, would not want him to do this thing with Ratna, no matter how many gold coins were offered. She would be hurt, but being the good wife she is she would try her best not to show it.

And it wasn't as if he was going to spoil a family girl, I reminded him. He was going to use Ratna exactly as I had raised her to be used.

He thought of himself, he thought of his wife, he thought of Ratna, but I don't think he thought about the child that was to come of this bargain. Only much, much later did it strike him with such force that here was a child with no father to care for her.

Durga

I sang the song with Periamma, and Kanaka stood up and tied the bells around her ankles, and smiled at me before she became her other self, her self that glows with all that's inside her, that can make gods, each in his own splendour. Drums beat like a heart for the whole world. Beings appear wherever she puts them with her fingers, thick forests with branches that block out the sun, snakes entwined, a river, the crescent moon, a bull with curved horns, which makes the earth shake as he paces. The gods look down, I see them; they throw flowers, I catch them. The demons look down too, and they are black, their teeth long. But then I can't watch; the more she danced, the more she became strange to me. The drum beat faster, the cymbals of the master broke the time into little pieces so that it no longer flowed, but stopped and started, slowed and hastened, and I couldn't stay where I was in it. The whole room fell into broken shards around me, and beings who'd been hidden came out from dark shadows. She became the wild god, her dancing made him dance, one foot stamping on the head of the demon, one leg raised, one hand in the gesture of benediction, one hand bursting into flames. I tried to keep my eyes fixed on her feet, for they were still her feet. I had to close my eyes, but I could still feel the web of glances coming from every direction and they held me pinned, the eyes left me and like hungry beasts roamed over her, opening and closing, one bite, swallowing her alive. Eyes like coal, black and burning hot, her pink skirt and blouse, her skin soft as petals was being burned by their hot eyes that leaked their evil, lust melting and flowing out of them over her and on to us all. Sharp eyes like knives cutting her up, burning discs, letting off sparks as they spun. So many eyes, sparkling and flashing. *Her* eyes flowed over all of us like honey. When I couldn't bear it any longer I ran away to hide from all those eyes, ran in the darkness through the strange house, where the sleeping bodies of servants lay on the floor in front of closed doors. I crawled finally into a pot like a womb, for storing rice, now emptied for the wedding feast.

Where the seven shallow granite steps are, no longer even, and the pillars that stood along one edge, all fallen down, there is where I sat. Kanaka said, stay here. She gave me a stick and said, find something pretty.

I tried not to look. I never turned towards the voices saying words. I looked only when the voices stopped, when the murmur of their voices became no more than the wind in the lacy leaves of the jacaranda tree, when they poured themselves from one to the other. I looked only for a moment because their naked bodies gave off such heat. Nothing stirred except for those two, and the insects, buzzing. Breath coming in gasps, her breath, my breath, whose breath? I covered my ears trying to keep their voices out, turned my eyes inward to see what was happening in the cave of my skull. Each time he took her, he took her further away from me, but each time she came back she was softer, more tender, more kind. I don't want her to go, I want her to be with me always. Kanaka is quick and I am slow. Kanaka has big eyes, like a doe's. If Kanaka goes, I follow.

I opened my mouth but nothing came out, nothing with any meaning attached. The crow made a sound, arw, arw, arw. She was pressed against the tree, his arm across her throat so she couldn't scream. Time didn't move as he tried to push his knee between her two knees, pressed together.

If only I could close my eyes, it would stop, but I couldn't do it. I had to go on seeing, and so it went on being done in front of me. If only I could close my eyes I could again become the centre, but I couldn't, and my self was leaving me through my eyes, entering her, entering him. She was hurt; he was hurting her. His eyes sliding like oil covered her, made it hard for her to breathe. The air, the air, she was gasping, gasping, choking, coughing. His eyes were so heavy on her, they weighed her down, she sank. I had to call her back, remind her again who she was. His gaze crawled all over her like a line of ants. She swayed, she fell. She was breaking apart into an inside and an outside, coming out through her eyes, through her ears and her mouth. She streamed out. I wanted to cover my ears, close my eyes and let the dark put a stop to it. But instead I made my own gaze hard, I pierced him with it, through the hard shell he flowed out loose and liquid. And then I said the words to wake her up, Ka na ka Ka na ka, I called her to come, to be mine again. I ran to hide.

Nattuvanar

When I had to remind her for the third time to pause before stamping, I said, 'What is wrong with you? You're thick as a plank today.' No doubt it is a complicated pattern, with that half beat before the thatimetu in thisra nadai going against the rhythm, until the tension breaks and dance and music flow together again. Difficult as it was, it had never caused her to falter before. Today, she couldn't seem to get beyond it. I should have said, 'Let's keep going. Tomorrow it will be all right. We should not dwell on this mistake, lest it become ingrained.' But instead of being gentle with her, I became stubborn. She made the same mistake again, and again. The seventh time I was so angry I hurled the thattakali at her. It bounced and struck her on the thigh, but I swear it could not have hurt her badly.

The correct response would have been for Kanaka to pick

up the stick and, bowing at my feet, ask for my forgiveness for her mistake before giving it back into my hand. When she was a child, this is what I required her to do. But it had been some time since I'd had to even mention an error. She noticed immediately when a stamp or a hasta or the lift of an eyebrow was imperfect, and corrected it herself without a word from me. Over the last few months she'd begun to dance with a lightness to her steps, an extra flourish that added to the beauty of her movements just as the dimple added to her smile. Yet every movement was precise, clear and rhythmic, like a line of classical Tamil etched with a sharp stylus on a palm leaf. Something had happened to her in the years of our practice together – like the clay becoming the pot, or the gold becoming the bangle, she had transmuted completely into the dances she performed. I said to Nagaveni, 'I am ready for anyone on earth to see her dance and pass judgement. Let's set a date for her arangetram.' Nagaveni was eager too, and chose an auspicious date. That date was now hardly a month away.

A guru can't shine on his own. He needs a student to shine for him. I had boasted of Kanaka to all the great nattuvanars. My own hopes and dreams were tied up in her. So when she told me what she'd done, I was in despair as much for the thwarting of my own dreams as for her.

I loved her, but it would be dishonest and arrogant on

my part to say I was like a father to her. Yet she was the living repository of all I know, so in that sense she was my daughter, since she contained my essence. But a guru is not a parent; no one who loved her in that way could have been as strict with her as I was, for this dance is not easy to learn. When I first came here six years ago, every day I took the dhavani she tied around her waist and used it to bind her to the pillar in aramandi position, legs a perfect square, so tight that she could not rise, and in that way I trained her through all the adavus. Thattu adavus in three kalas, without stopping, and if she stopped, we started all over again from the first, and we went on in this way until she could do all eight without a pause. I didn't relent even when tears filled her eyes, and her thighs trembled from the effort. Muscles only learn through pain. If she made a mistake I rapped her palm with the long handle of a brass spoon heated in the embers. Once it was so hot that her skin burned in a strip, and blistered. How she hated me, hated this dance, in those early days! But I loved her through all this, and I gave her all the great beauty I had in my family, gave her what she alone was able to take. But that isn't right either. I gave her the wood, she set it on fire, making heat, making warmth. I taught other dancers, and Ratna too, but they danced as if my gift was a burden of heavy logs they carried.

Knowing her as a student is not really knowing her. She

had to put herself aside when she came to me. The steps, the hastas, the body positions, when she concentrated on those she was able to distance herself from anything that might be bothering her, or making her angry or sad. That's how dance becomes an addiction, like any other – opium, liquor, cards, women – letting you forget your troubles for the duration of its hold over you.

When she and I were perfectly attuned, her foot hit the floor with a crisp slap that perfectly matched the sound of my stick on the wood block. That day the sound her feet made was flat and heavy. So I should have known there was a problem, and treated her more gently.

Instead, I shouted, 'And where's Ganapathy? He needs the practice more than you. Why doesn't he come at least on those days when he's in the village?'

She stumbled to the corner of the room that can't be seen from the doorway, and wept, shaken by sobs, as if every hope in the world was gone. I got up and went to console her, and she slid to the floor all curled at my feet. I said, 'I'm an old man now, but I was also young once. Nothing can be as bad as all that. You can tell me. I'm your grandfather.'

I saw it was not an easy story for her to tell, here in this room where anyone walking by might overhear. Nagaveni amma was the one I worried about. She's sharp. She would have been the first to question the why and the wherefore of our stopping the practice, but luckily she'd gone to a neighbouring village for her own work and would not be back for some hours. I sent Kanaka to the well at the back to wash her face, then took her by the narrow outside stair to the upper veranda with the fretted windows, where the lovely women of this house can watch processions and the goings-on of the street without being stared at by every common man. It is the most private space in this very public house.

When we were alone, slowly in bits and pieces, she confessed the reason for her distress. Everything, what Ganapathy had done to her, and what had happened to him. I said, 'This is no fault of yours. Ganapathy brought it on himself by his behaviour.' I knew Ganapathy's habits well, how many women he'd screwed, wives and sisters and daughters of men, any one of whom could have done this deed. I told her all this. I said, 'The hairpin! Surely you took your hairpin?' In the turmoil of the moment she had forgotten it.

It was such a pretty thing, and other females would have noticed and envied both the design of the parakeet and Kanaka's hair, thick enough to support a heavy silver stick like that.

If not for the hairpin, there was nothing tying her to his death. It had to be retrieved. If she couldn't do it, at least I could make her show me where the body was so I could get it. She took me to the back gate of the temple garden. It looked as if the rusted padlock could never be opened, the latch itself rusted into place. 'If you expect me to climb over that, I can't manage it,' I said. She had no such expectation. Instead, she lifted the gate by its crossbeam, and opened it easily by the other side. The pin through the hinges had been removed, and it was easy enough to go through and rest it back as it had been. No one looking at the gate would realize it had been opened in the last ten years.

I left her there and went on alone. The body was exactly where she'd described, slumped against the tree. I felt a wave of pity for Ganapathy when I saw how, with the life gone out like a light, the flesh of his once-handsome face sagged and hung loose over the bones of his face. His muscular legs were stretched out in front of him, his dhoti and komanam soaked in blood and in disarray. There, high up on his thigh was the small round wound from where the blood had flowed out of him, but the hairpin itself was nowhere to be found.

Kanaka trembled when I told her. 'Someone who means me harm must have taken it. Someone knows.'

I feared Vallabendran finding out. He was the law of the land here, and if it came to his attention that Ganapathy was dead and Kanaka was responsible, he would make assumptions about the nature of their relationship that would nullify Kanaka's value to him. I pointed out the danger to her. 'If Vallabendran's interest in you turns to disgust, he may be happy to toss you to the police. It is easy enough for him to direct their attention wherever he wants it to go. Tell Nagaveni amma. She won't like what you've done, she'll scold you, but she'll know how to manage the situation.' But she refused. I gathered from her reluctance that she had her own plan of which Nagaveni would disapprove. I had no idea what that was, I didn't want to know. Anything I knew, Nagaveni would have got out of me, I wouldn't be able to dissemble in front of her. If anyone asked me whether I knew where Kanaka was, I could answer, honestly, no. I did gather this, that her plan depended on the help of some man. I wanted to tell her that men and their words can't be trusted, especially not the ones they say when trying to get a girl to open her legs. But I kept the thought to myself. Maybe there is one such man who means what he says in the throes of passion.

The terrain of love is not a grassy meadow. It is rocky, thorny, inhabited by snakes and scorpions.

I concealed Ganapathy's disappearance with a lie, that's all. That man got only what he deserved, and I told her I would feel no remorse on his account, and neither should she. I know Ganapathy through and through. Some may say he is a good drummer, but I for one am not much taken with that flashy style, throwing his hands around, making a big show of arriving on the sam as if it is an accomplishment rather than the most basic requirement that the drummer must fulfil. Rhythm is inbuilt in me, I feel it, I don't need to count, so I wasn't impressed by his cheap tricks. I have command over all the talas and the nadais, and in the Suladi I had composed for Kanaka's arangetram, each of the eight verses is in a different tala complicated further with different nadais in each one. The patterns I invented were for her alone, only she could have performed that dance. Ganapathy depended on her, not the other way round, as it should have been.

Ganapathy spent more on the perfumed oil he used to grease his curls than he gave to his wife. Only the ugly girls of our caste marry. With her flat nose and thick lips like a camel's, she must have been pleased to have got herself such a handsome husband. But she's learned through bitter experience how little his face reflected his character. Looks mean nothing when the man's never home but always out somewhere seducing whichever woman happens to have caught his eye. Ganapathy's silk shirts and ruby ear studs and the gold rings on his fingers came at his wife's expense, and if Nagaveni hadn't held back part of his payment and given it directly to her, she'd have had nothing to run the household on.

What I did was only this – I asked that wife of his to pack a bag for him with his good shirt and veshti for a performance in Thirunelveli, and, holding out five rupees, I said, 'He asked me to advance you this from his share of the payment.' She took it quickly from my hand and asked no more questions.

I left the bag on the train, so some lucky railway porter would get a fancy veshti with a red-and-gold brocade border and some shirts. I had a pleasant stay with relatives in Thirunelveli, and came back after two days. By the time I returned, what with the statue's appearance in the temple and Kanaka's mysterious disappcarance, Ganapathy's wife questioned me at length, asking me for details of the concert and, of course, wanting to know where he was. Why had I returned but not Ganapathy? Since everyone is well aware of his habits, I said, 'I don't know. He said he had more concerts, but the details he didn't share with me.' Why should he, after all? He is notorious for going his own way, not accountable to anyone. The wife knows that. As to the imagined performance, I made up a very passable account that would be difficult to verify without going to Thirunelveli, which I doubt anyone will have the determination to do. After all, I know the place well.

'But he gave me thirty rupees to give you for the household expenses while he's away,' I said, and it was a rare delight to see the conflicting emotions play on her face – desire for the money, reluctance to abandon her accusations against

Kanaka, that she'd seduced him and they'd run off together. Finally the money won, and she grabbed the notes from my hand and knotted them into the pallav of her sari.

I'm only a nattuvanar, and an old man without friends or family. I came at Nagaveni's request and I stay here by her grace. She in her great erudition recognized the value of the repertoire of songs and dances passed on to me by my father who had been related by marriage to someone in her mother's family. So our relationship was, is, close. I wouldn't have done what I did if I had thought that it would bring Kanaka to any harm.

Luckily for me, Nagaveni expressed no suspicions at all about my story, she was so distraught. When, away from listening ears, for in front of others she expressed no doubt about the miracle, she asked me, 'Do you have any idea where my darling is, did she say anything at all to you?' I could say no with perfect honesty glowing from my eyes.

Now, without a doubt, Nagaveni loved Kanaka, but at the same time, her own grandiose plans depended on her, so it was not an unselfish love, if such there is. As the girl had grown more beautiful of face and form, and with her exceptional dancing ability along with a natural grace and charm, Nagaveni had convinced herself that Kanaka, with the right push and the right circumstances, could catch the eye of someone high in the firmament, a wealthy and influential patron, a raja even. A courtesan is like a balance, she tilts to the side that has more gold.

The problem was Vallabendran. He's also a raja, but that's just what every zamindar likes to be called, and for him it is more a title of polite respect than a mark of royalty such as someone like the raja of Puddukottai or the raja of Travancore commands. Vallabendran had been Nagaveni's patron, and then when Ratna came of age, he'd moved with no trouble at all from mother to daughter. Now that the younger daughter had reached puberty, what was to stop him from making her next in line? He wasn't held in check by the thought that she might be his own child. Our raja is not used to having his desires denied for any reason. Anyway, the child of a devadasi is fatherless, for no one really knows how devadasis conduct their lives in private. They live in great intimacy with musicians and nattuvanars, and if there are liaisons, the patron, if he is wise, overlooks what it is not within his power to prevent. My own experiences confirm that clever men and charming women in close proximity look to each other for pleasure and companionship.

But I stayed away from such speculation. What I do know is how his interest was first aroused. He saw her dance at a wedding, where she should never have danced at all. She was sitting next to Nagaveni, and singing alongside her while Ratna and girls of lesser calibre danced. A rasika in the gathering said, 'Let Kanaka dance. I've heard that she is very good.' Nagaveni tried her best to deflect him, but she couldn't do so without being rude. Finding no way to avoid the situation, Nagaveni chose for Kanaka a purely devotional padam, not even slightly provocative.

The song was in Bhairavi, describing Shiva in procession. Kanaka showed his terrifying form – his necklace of snakes, his matted locks piled high on his head, the river Ganga caught therein and sparkling like diamonds, his sacred ash-smeared arms and chest and forehead, clothed in tiger skin and riding on Nandi, his magnificent bull. In the procession came dancers, she showed their leaps and turns, men blowing curved horns, drummers, beating and stamping and spinning with the drums slung around their necks. We had worked out with the harmonium player a little trick, where the moment when she mimed holding the horn to her lips and blowing, he with perfect timing squeezed out a long note that sounded forth exactly like a horn. The audience broke into spontaneous clapping, so much so that we had to repeat the same trick. So Vallabendran not only saw how she had grown up, but witnessed the high praise and adulation she received. For a man like him, that was almost a provocation. He wanted her first, before any other man could get his chance.

When Nagaveni realized that Vallabendran was not

deterred from pursuing Kanaka, she went to great lengths to keep the girl from crossing his line of vision again. Kanaka was prevented from going out during the day, ostensibly so that the harsh rays of the sun didn't darken her perfect skin, but really to prevent Vallabendran's lustful gaze burning her up. She wasn't allowed to go to Ratna's house, as she was likely to run into him there. She no longer accompanied Nagaveni when she got a troupe together to perform. Nagaveni's most powerful objection to Vallabendran was that Kanaka had not gone through the ceremony of dedication to the deity of the temple that made her available to men. And in this the law had recently changed in her favour. Dedication was no longer considered an honourable life for a woman, so the ritual could not be done with a child. The girl had to be sixteen at least, and Kanaka still had a few months before she reached that age. Until then Nagaveni was refusing to proceed with the dedication ceremony. Within this time she'd conduct Kanaka's arangetram in the grand manner that would attract the attention of someone more suited to her growing ambitions.

Vallabendran is a man of the world. He understood that Nagaveni was putting obstacles in the path of his desire for Kanaka for her own reasons, for he was a law unto himself, and no one would have dared to bring up legalities if Nagaveni had prepared Kanaka and gone through the rituals in the village temple. But it was not clear to me what his intentions were. Sometimes he seemed uninterested in making the next move, and at other times he seemed to be determined that no one else should have a claim to Kanaka's first night.

I have no idea where the gold statue came from, or how it got into the sanctum sanctorum. Maybe this was all part of Kanaka's plan. If so she is greater even than I thought. This is the best possible outcome, that she should disappear into a statue of gold. Now even if Ganapathy's dead body is found, no one will blame her, it will only add to her glory. Like Kannagi, also golden, who tore off her own breast and, with the power residing in it, burned Madurai when the king of that city wrongly killed her husband. Some take a devadasi as no better than a prostitute, but the power of her chastity is equal to that of the wedded wife.

I will not dispute that. I am an old man, what do I know? Still it saddens me that great patrons of the arts will not see her dance as my student, and she will not show the beauty of this art to the whole world. And even more than that, I grieve that I will not see her perfect mandi adavu one more time. If you saw her distracted from milking the cow by the sound of Krishna's flute, you'd hear the haunting tune yourself. If you saw her whisper into the ear of her sakhi, you would see that friend standing just there, beside her. And if she mimed writing a letter to her lover, but finding no words folded up and sent to him just the tears that had fallen on the page, you'd be pierced by such loneliness.

Medical Examiner's Report – Form No. 289

The body was brought to my office covered in a thin homespun cloth and wrapped in bamboo matting. Accompanied by the police constable, four Doms on foot had carried it over a distance of more than eighty miles in this heat and humidity. So you may imagine for yourself the condition of the body. It was very trying and disgusting to conduct the post-mortem and while it was well within my rights to refuse in these circumstances, I proceeded to make as thorough an examination as practicable purely from a desire to offer some clue as to the cause and manner of death.

Decomposition had progressed to the point of putrefaction, and moving maggots were found in eyes, nose and mouth as well as in other body cavities. Bloating had caused severe distortion of the face and body. Skin was diffusely coloured greenish black and the epidermis had separated from the underlying dermis. It was difficult to make a conclusive judgement, but it seemed as if there was evidence of the feeding activity of some small marine animal, perhaps turtles.

The only article of clothing was a long skirt gathered and tied tightly at the waist. It showed no signs of blood or semen, but that is only to be expected, given that the body was in the water for an estimated time of two weeks.

Along with minor signs, such as nose-ring aperture in left nostril and three openings along the helix of both ears for ornaments, the presence of the uterus, resistant as it is to putrefaction, establishes without a doubt that the corpse is female. Hair had separated due to skin slippage, but it was 2 feet 7 inches long, black, thick and somewhat wavy.

No attempt was made to obtain fingerprints, given that the epidermal separation had progressed to degloving. There was no necessity for identifying and packing the bulb of the fingers, as there was no indication of her being a habitual criminal.

The union of epiphyses and bone in sternum, clavicle, femur and first and second sacral vertebrae leads me to estimate the age of the victim as over 25 and under 40.

Viscera bottles with pieces of liver, kidney and spleen were sent to the chemical examiner. Small intestine, being already full of maggots, was not sent. No evidence was found of arsenic, datura or aconite. Since the list of poisons easily available in the market is almost infinite, the absence of these three is an indeterminate rather than negative result.

There are indications that strangulation with a thin rope may have been the cause of death. It is equally possible that it was a blow to the head. Nor has some form of poison been ruled out. All I can say for sure is that it was not drowning, since she was already dead when thrown into the well.

I consider that the cause of death cannot be established definitively through a medical examination of a body in this state of decomposition. As N. Chevers stated so clearly in his manual on medical jurisprudence for India, the calm, timid surface of the native hides a nature that combines sensuality, jealousy, a gift for lying, superstitions of the most outrageous kind and a disregard for human life that is at times shocking. Theft, kidnapping, assassination, abortion, adultery, rape and murder, sometimes for the most trivial of reasons, are common crimes. Only a thorough investigation into the circumstances, preferably through some agent familiar with the people of the village, will lead to a more definite conclusion. While making these inquiries, it is important to remember that those who identified the body wrongly as a young girl of fourteen may have good reason to conceal the real facts.

Janardana

Janardana stepped naked out of the bathroom. He wrapped one thin towel around his shoulder-length curly hair, twisted and twisted it into a long coil, which he wrapped and knotted on his head like a bun. He took from the hook on the wall another towel, but before draping it around his waist, he admired himself in the mirror. His chin was smooth, his cheeks plump and round, his lips reddened by betel. He pushed his penis back, in between his thighs and arranged his legs, one slightly forward and modestly close, as a shy maiden might stand. He was plump enough that his nipples and small breasts too, plucked free of all hair by the barber, were as big as a girl's. He inhaled, sucking in his stomach and puffing out his chest, and admired the effect he'd created. He'd been doing this for years, whenever he was alone in his room. He pouted at his reflection, making seductive faces, turning his head in one direction, then the other, talking to himself in a high, breathy voice as if he were someone else entirely.

Even as a child, he'd been soft and feminine, though he hadn't known then that he should hide it. The aunties and grandmothers had doted on him, putting ribbons in his hair, laughing and clapping when he sang in his baby voice the grown-up love songs they taught him. It was only as a young boy who didn't like to sit on walls and pass lewd remarks about the young girls who walked to market or church or temple that he learned ways of keeping his desires secret while revealing them too. First an uncle, and then one of his teachers and after that an older cousin had shown him what could be accomplished in a few stolen moments together in a stairwell or a storeroom or a dark back lane. When he grew older he went after men more to his taste – not men who fucked men, but men who fucked women, who were married or went to prostitutes. He was careful with this side of himself. Though he suspected that many in his family knew his predilections, they had enough of the sense of their own position in the world to never speak of it or acknowledge any whispers they might have heard. No one had ever suggested to him that he was not a good candidate for marriage, even though by then another uncle and a couple more cousins and a sister's husband had let him do what he wanted in secret, in the dark, pretending to be asleep. When the time came, they arranged his marriage. They trusted him to know, as they did, that in families like his the most important thing was not his private actions, but the face and persona he presented to the outside world.

Of all the people within his circle, only Ratna had ever watched him transform into his other, most secret self, beautiful and desirable. In fact, only by Ratna's active intervention could he have made real those dreams he hardly knew he had. One day he'd been in her room as she dressed herself in expectation of Vallabendran's arrival. He'd stood behind her and looked into the mirror, becoming so immersed in her reflection that his own sense of standing and watching vanished into that image. He became the one who, with a little finger dipped into the filigreed silver locket shaped like a mango, limned long eyes with kajal, who with mobile, elegant fingers chose between diamond and ruby and inserted it expertly into the tiny hole in a curved nostril, who adjusted coral and pearls in a tight circle around a slender neck. 'Let me do your hair,' he'd said, and he'd dipped his fingers into the bowl of castor oil scented with sandalwood, rubbed it into her long, lustrous hair from root to tip as if it were his own, braided it expertly, arranged it into a bun, all the while looking into the mirror. The fragrance of jasmine, the flowers from her own garden just picked and woven together tightly into a thick strand, intoxicated him as he wrapped it neatly at her nape and fixed it with hairpins. Ratna held up her hand mirror to admire the effect, but it was his face she had framed when she said, 'How well you do that, Janardana.' Their eyes met in the glass, and she saw, before he could disguise it, his hungry look. She beckoned him to sit beside her. 'You've got the softness of a girl, Janardana, and so many womanly skills. Now it's my turn to dress you up. I can make a very pretty and seductive creature out of you.' She played it like a game, and he gave in as if to her caprice, while knowing full well that she was acting upon a desire within him so deep and intense that he had so far not even dared to let it enter his consciousness, but had kept it as his own most intimate secret. She turned to face him, while he remained gazing into the mirror, in a trance. 'I wager that I can turn you into Mohini,' she said, 'for, if Vishnu can be so transformed, why not you?'

Janardana had often thought the very same thing himself, that there were so many stories he'd been told or seen enacted in dance dramas about male gods and kings and mere ordinary mortals, either of their own volition or through some random circumstance, changing into women.

In the Puranas, Arunan, charioteer of the sun god, became a woman twice, so he must have liked the feeling. Or in the Matsya Purana, where King Ila becomes a woman by entering a forest grove sacred to Parvathi, and then asks of Shiva the boon that he be male for one month and female the next. Such an arrangement, Janardana thought, would suit him as well.

Ratna began, as she'd done for herself, with the kajal, taking a smudge of it on her ring finger, pulling down his lower lid and smearing the thick black unguent along the inner rim. She looked critically at the effect, then extended the line at the corners into an upward sweep that dramatically changed the look of his eyes, the whites whiter, the dark pupils bigger and more demanding of attention. She took a pair of iron tweezers and plucked a few thick dark stray hairs from his eyebrows. 'Not too much or your wife will notice. How is she by the way? You should make sure she's satisfied, or she'll have a valid reason to stray.' Ratna's voice stayed sweet, so Janardana couldn't tell if the words were friendly advice or meant to needle. He didn't need to be reminded that it had been months since he'd gone to visit his wife in his ancestral home. He had done his best to do his duty by his wife, but after the first daughter and the second had been born, without much in the way of input from him, he only visited his wife to avoid any scandal should she be successful in her ongoing efforts with a handsome servant to have a son.

Ratna tied his thick curls back and attached a false braid

that she used for dance. Since the fresh jasmine already decorated her own hair, she took out the flowers of pith that would deceive anyone from a distance.

'How should I wrap your sari? None of my blouses will fit you, so I'll have to do it in the way of women who don't wear blouses. A nine-yard one, so you look like a Brahmin lady? Or with the pleat in the back, like a farm maiden, all dressed up to celebrate the harvest festival? I think that will be better. That way, I can show off your hairless calves and slender ankles.' She didn't ask his opinion on which sari, but held up a pink, and then a green and finally a turquoise blue, as if to check which one better complemented his complexion, while gauging, without seeming to, the pleasure of his response. He could hardly take his eyes off his image in the mirror with one sari after another held up against his skin.

'Are you naturally so hairless or do you get the barber to pluck off the body hair from your back and arms and armpits? I like rough, dark, hairy men, so you wouldn't please me in bed.' And that was just the kind of man Janardana liked as well. Ratna pleated one end of the sea green sari she'd chosen and placed the fan at his hips, knotted it, wound the sari all the way round him, then folded it up and across his chest and over the left shoulder and back round to be tucked in the front. Now when he looked at himself in the mirror, with the drape of the sari obscuring his chest and what hung between his legs still, he saw his inner vision of himself made visible.

'Go on, go out and take a round of the house. See if anyone looks twice, or notices your good looks enough to make an approach. Go on! Don't pretend to be so shy. You're really still a man after all.'

And so it had begun. He'd go to Ratna's house, knowing already from their conversations that Vallabendran had no plan to visit her, dress himself in her clothes and go out in the evenings, just as the sun began to set. He'd already perfected a feminine walk with a slight sway of the hips. In this dress, he wouldn't dare to look among his own caste, even should he want to, for the risk of being discovered and reviled was too great. But that was irrelevant because his preference was the hard, muscular men of the labouring lower castes. It added an extra element of humiliation and degradation that he found heightened his pleasure. He'd make his way to a place where one or other of the field workers and day labourers could be found hanging around after they'd finished their evening's emptying of bowels in the fields and were looking for someone to give them quick relief of another kind. 'Give me some betel from your bag.' 'In my bag, the betel nut is so big, are you sure it can enter your mouth?' And so the conversation would start, becoming more lewd by degrees until the man said, 'Why not give me what I want, since my taking it will not diminish it in any way. You'll have just as much to offer.' They would follow him, watching his bum, along a path behind the bushes. This was always a moment of danger, when the man might try to put his hand underneath the sari, between Janardana's legs, but he would pre-empt such attempts by dropping to his knees and getting to the man's treasure first with his mouth. Once he got started, no man ever complained.

In his normal attire and in his position as Vallabendran's brother-in-law, he might encounter the man again. How ironic it was that he'd knelt at the feet of the low-caste man who now stood before him with head bent. No matter how hungry or thirsty he was, he'd never be able to accept food or water from him, yet he'd already swallowed something far more polluting. It was the hypocrisy practised by all men of good caste, that while they raised the legs of untouchable girls on to their shoulders, they wouldn't take food from their hands. Yet both sides knew, didn't they, that in the privacy of their desire, they'd been equals.

Janardana didn't care for Kanaka one way or the other, despite that golden complexion and the dimple, her joyful nature and her skill at dance. He had watched her grow up, doted upon by everyone from babyhood, and had noticed how Nagaveni basked in that reflected glory. He knew that people saw no guile in her, but recently he himself was not so sure. So habituated to keeping his own secret, he recognized signs that she was hiding something in her always pleasing manner and polite speech. He supposed that she had a lover somewhere, but the only candidate seemed to be the handsome drummer Ganapathy. Janardana's loyalty was to Ratna, and in supporting her, he even stood against Vallabendran, dissuading him at every opportunity from casting Ratna aside in favour of Kanaka.

Ratna had no one else to whom she could express her anger at the way Kanaka was coddled, so she often unburdened herself to Janardana. 'God knows she's always had it her way. Whatever she wants, Nagaveni has given her. Praise? What part of her hasn't been praised? As if I don't have eyes too, and long eyelashes. The girl is going to give Nagaveni a real headache one day, you'll see. Now, watch, she'll suffer, and I'll smile behind my hand.' Janardana listened to Ratna but more than that he watched her, memorizing her gestures, storing them away for the moment he could take on her persona along with her clothes. 'I was only thirteen. Ripe enough, Nagaveni thought, but now look how she's delaying the proceedings for Kanaka, when she is already a full two years older. I lay under a man, I screamed in pain, I bore a child, but now Kanaka doesn't have to do any of those things. She is allowed to dance all day, she is not branded with the mark of this temple. It irks me that Nagaveni won't do anything about it.'

He recognized that Kanaka's ascendance was damaging Ratna. 'Do you fear losing Vallabendran to her? What will you do if he is determined to be her patron?'

'Vallabendran is a man. Do I really need to say more? He wants what he wants when he wants it. I'm not sure that he cares whether Kanaka is his child. In the meantime he knows our ways. He knows what he is paying for, but I'm not sure he realizes that his desires may have been ignited by someone else. Nagaveni is the one who taught him the ways of finding pleasure. She even taught him how to get on with his new young wife. Poor Devayani! I know she's your sister, but really, the way Nagaveni had her scared! Imagine, her husband's mistress was the one who came to remove the evil eye when her son Indra was born. Nagaveni was right in the middle of that marriage, and for all I know it may have been to the good, since she had a vested interest in keeping both sides happy.

'When Vallabendran was a young man, knowing about women only what Nagaveni had put into his head, he never for a moment doubted my virginity. When he first came to my bed, it was easy enough to struggle and squirm and keep my thighs pressed together and cry out, just at the right moment, as if with a sharp pain. The bladder of goat's blood was pierced and spilled to stain the sheet, but Vallabendran hardly noticed, so taken was he by kissing away my tears. He didn't leave until he'd had me again, and not without putting gold bangles on to each wrist to distract me and stop my wailing.'

'Going from mother to daughter was not a problem for him?'

'Why should it be? Don't the poems say that the man who's paying can choose: the experience and skilful lovemaking of the mother, the beauty and freshness of the daughter, or the untasted sweetness of the granddaughter?

'Nagaveni had seen his eyes wandering towards me and she took the steps she deemed appropriate. I don't blame her. She let him know that she didn't mind too much if, like the bee looking for honey, he wandered from flower to flower as long as he stayed in the same garden. So we could retain our offices and payment from the temple, supplemented by the gifts and prestige that accrued through his patronage. Nagaveni was loath to give up any of that.

'I had no strong objection. I'd seen him coming and going from childhood, heard him with Nagaveni behind closed doors, seen him take one or other of the girls of the household when Nagaveni was indisposed. I'd even entered the room with his freshly washed clothes or a pitcher of water or the spittoon. I saw and envied a little the pretty gifts he gave Nagaveni, and how languorous and contented she looked when the door opened again after many hours, and how he slept on and on into the late afternoon.

'But something about coming to the mother's house to screw the daughter, when he'd screwed the mother for such a good long time, must have made him uncomfortable. That's how I got this house, when it fell into his lap as repayment for a debt. Since it was not on his property and not within the village where Nagaveni would have full knowledge of his visits, but here on this side road, easily accessible no matter in which direction he was travelling, he equipped it suitably and made it over to me.'

'What will you do if Vallabendran really does become the patron of Kanaka?'

'I have no complaints about Vallabendran. He has been generous with me, giving me silver anklets with two rows of bells, and then silver anklets with no bells at all, at my whim of the moment. He took pleasure in the pleasure that a ring or a nose jewel gave me, and I was always quick to show my gratitude. When we go on singing and dancing about love, it seems as if we should know what it is. But really all we know is how to simulate it, stage it, act it out. We are like the decoys set out by hunters to attract the wild ducks into their nets. Many birds are caught, but we ourselves never fly. Nagaveni always taught me that real love undermines our love play.

Real love fades, it becomes stale and repetitious. The woman paid for her services does a better job of pleasing a man and keeping him in her thrall because she can exercise her skills uncomplicated by real emotion. The less she feels the more easily she is able to enact it – it's an art, like any other. A woman with perfect breasts is not an artist, but the sculptor who carves the perfect breast is. So if Vallabendran has tired of me and chooses now to go to Kanaka, I have no means to stop him, though it makes me feel a kind of sadness I did not expect. I thought it was all play, with wooden weapons, but in the end I may have put into Vallabendran's hands a real sword. How will I not lose the battle?'

'But at least tell me that's not what you want.'

'How could it be? Where am I to go?'

'Yes, we are both entirely dependent on Vallabendran's goodwill.'

Ratna had told him about Vallabendran's impotence and how it worried her. She wondered aloud whether some sacrifice needed to be made, a goat or a pig, or some ritual that could only be performed by a magician she trusted, a gaunt, toothless man with strange grey eyes, since all the remedies she'd tried had yielded no success. 'I mean to try and find him right away, to take advantage of the power of the new moon's first light. I may be reciting the mantra he gives me, but you can do what you like all night.'

So he did. He dressed up, went out, found a man to his tastes, and then another and another. It was late when he returned. He walked cautiously along the side road in case Vallabendran, or anyone else who could embarrass him, had come unexpectedly. Ratna was the only person he trusted.

He heard voices. One he recognized as Ratna's but of the identity of the other voice he wasn't sure. He didn't dare enter the house, not dressed like this, and rather than walk into the presence of someone who might betray him, he crouched underneath the closed window and tried to identify the speaker. He could hardly make out any words, but the tone of Ratna's voice conveyed worry, irritation and even anger. The other voice, very hushed, was the one doing most of the talking. Something should have been hidden but it wasn't and somewhere there was a trail of blood. Then Ratna said clearly, 'Why didn't you tell him?' He couldn't hear the answer, and nothing they said gave a clue as to who the 'him' that should have been told was. After the long and unintelligible reply came again the question from Ratna, 'But then how did he find out?' and to this the other voice wailed, 'I don't know! I don't know! I don't even know if he did find out. All I know is that he didn't come. And now what am I to do?' For a while there was only the sound of the girl's sobs and Ratna saying something like 'don't cry, dear, don't cry, it will be all right'. He guessed that the crying girl was

Kanaka, and it surprised him that Ratna was so gentle, when she'd seemed so hard set against her.

'Did he give you any money?'

There was the word 'jewels' in the answer to that question, and Janardana could imagine the bright, avaricious light that came into Ratna's eyes with that word.

'Well, this is more than enough. He has treated you with honour and respect.'

Now the voices went back and forth in argument and, despite Ratna's more forceful and insistent tone, it seemed as if Kanaka with quiet determination was winning. Finally Ratna said quite loudly, 'Then have it your own way. I'll grind the roots. You take the medicine now and get it over with. It is painful, but all of us have gone through it, so why not you too?' That much was clear. The so innocent girl had a lover and now she was suffering the usual complaint. No surprise there. Nagaveni's own fault for not conducting her puberty ceremony and finding her a patron, and such a pretty girl at that. Still, that was not so much cause for concern. What was it that should have been better hidden? Was that the thing that left a trail of blood? And who had given Kanaka jewels, and hadn't come because of something Kanaka should have told him before he himself found out?

The darkness, which when he'd arrived at Ratna's house showed only dark outlines, now showed that those shapes had leaves and twigs and branches. It would soon be daybreak. Before it was fully light, the village women would be making their way into the fields to do their morning business, and soon after that the men. So there was nothing to be done now. In case Janardana could be of assistance, he wanted Ratna to know she could call on him, but that must wait. He needed to get home unseen. Janardana quietly and carefully unpinned the flowers, unknotted the false braid and shook loose his own curls. He stripped off necklace and earrings, bangles and anklets. He made a little pile of everything he'd borrowed from Ratna's dressing table and stuffed it into the lamp niche on the side of the door. He unwrapped the sari, standing there only in his komanam while with one edge he wiped away the kajal around his eyes and the kumkum in the parting of his hair. Then he retied the sari as a dhoti. It was a strange colour for a man's garment, but if he got back while it was still dark no one would see him to remark on that. He realized he'd have to sneak it back to Ratna unwashed, lest the dhobi put it into Devayani's cupboard. She would be sure to notice and make a fuss. He tied a knot into the sari's end to remind himself before tucking it in at the waist, and headed home.

He walked along, watchful and alert as the darkness imperceptibly lightened, remembering a conversation from the previous afternoon that, in the light of the words he'd just heard, took on a new relevance. The boy Indra had just been handed a note by a servant from Nagaveni's household. 'What communication do you have with the devadasi's household?' Janardana had asked. 'I would have thought your tastes too modern for such relations.' Indra replied defensively, 'Some are different from others. They are not all mercenary, or lewd, or promiscuous.' 'Yes, I know, some are very pretty,' and at that he'd become almost laughably tongue-tied, stuttering something about how times were changing. 'So you've lost your heart to one already!' 'And so what if I have? Father says it is a mark of distinction.' 'I seem to remember that when you'd first come back from England you expressed some very different opinions and scorned our "feudal ways" as you called them.' 'It's different from what I thought it would be,' Indra had said, almost to himself, and the expression on his face as he said it was very raw and vulnerable. Janardana felt compelled to warn him, 'Be careful, that's all. The devadasis start learning their tricks right out of the womb.' 'She's never asked me for a thing.' 'And yet she took it, did she not, whatever you gave? They know how to get what they want without asking.' Indra was reading the note that the maid had handed him, and that last remark seemed to have missed him entirely, for he looked exultant. Janardana said, 'And you don't begrudge her any of it, I'll wager. It's said with good reason, "Of what use are these hands, if I can't caress her, these lips if I can't drink in her sweetness." I can see from your face that you know what I mean. Just make sure it's not the one your father's after – Kanaka. Everyone says that she's his child, which would make her your sister. It doesn't seem to bother him, but I have the feeling it would bother a modern boy with new ideas of how the world should be. She's the prettiest one, though, with her golden skin and that dimple.'

He'd said the words without any clear intention, and could easily have reassured the boy that there was every reason to think they weren't true if only he'd known. He walked the rest of the way home wondering if there was any way to undo the damage he'd done.

Ratna

'Are you sure you're pregnant?' Ratna asked. 'I missed my period, and my breasts are sore and swollen.' 'And you are determined to be rid of the child?' 'Yes.' 'Then I will prepare the medicine for that. But be warned, it is a terrible pain you'll have to bear, for it kills the child by almost killing you.' 'You've survived it.' 'Yes, and that is why I warn you, have the child.' 'No, that I can't do. I'll take the medicine.' The girl held her gaze, until finally Ratna shook her head in exasperation and considered what to say next, but finding no words that hadn't already been said, went to the puja room and came back with a blue cloth bag. She shook out from it several pieces of dried, shrivelled roots. Picking out three pieces, each about the size of a thumb, she pounded them into powder in the mortar and pestle, putting all the force of her frustration into the task. She mixed the powder with water in a tumbler and held it out to Kanaka. 'The taste is bitter and astringent, so swallow it as quickly as you can. You must keep it down. If you vomit, no good can come of it. And it will make you very sick, for two or three days, so resign yourself to the pain, and don't complain, since it's what you wanted.' She watched as Kanaka drained the glass, coughing and almost gagging but forcing herself to swallow it back down with a grimace. 'Good girl. Now try to sleep, so the first hours of pain are dulled.'

Kanaka moved to the rosewood plank, wide as a bed, that hung from the ceiling by four brass chains and lay down, saying, 'Oh, how I wish this long night would end. I'm afraid to sleep, in case I dream . . . of that.' Her smile as she said the words came as the real revelation of her sorrow, more so than her earlier tears. 'Oh, dear girl, what a thorny path you've chosen to walk,' Ratna said, and sat down too, taking Kanaka's head on her lap and setting the swing gently in motion with her foot.

Finally the rocking motion and the drug put the girl to sleep. Ratna traced with a finger the smooth arch of her brow and the gentle swell of her cheek. The gesture looked maternal but her expression was appraising, as one testing a pearl or silk or a mango to judge its quality – how much would a man pay who'd seen the dimple appear, and now wanted to find its golden hiding place? She could name her price and there would be someone ready to give good money to feel what her hand was feeling, to possess this tenderness and show it off once in a while to other men.

They were mother and daughter, the girl a piece of her. The qualities that everyone praised in Kanaka were Ratna's as well – Kanaka had her own petal-shaped eyes, her own heart-shaped face, her own slender figure, tiny waist, small, supple breasts. The dark Vallabendran and the hefty Nagaveni could never have produced this gift of a girl. No wonder Vallabendran was not satisfied by that story and wouldn't leave Kanaka alone. The long, thick hair, of course, was a feature of Nagaveni's lineage, shared by the three of them. Kanaka's fair skin was the gilding that made the features they had in common more radiant, more remarked, more valued. And that dimple, well, it caused a kind of pang, didn't it, the way it appeared and disappeared with her smile? A desire to see it again. All these were blessings that had come to Kanaka without any effort on her part, bestowed by the priest. In that sense, it was better that the girl was no one's, since the way she'd come into existence, if it came to be known, would dull her lustre. But it was almost eight years now since the priest had left the village, and others had no reason to remember him as vividly as Ratna did.

Nagaveni had paid him in gold for what spilled out of him so easily. The baby, finally pushed and pulled out from between Ratna's legs, had been called Kanaka for that reason, conceived as she'd been out of gold. The priest had been paid for his services, but not Ratna. Surely she deserved something.

Could Kanaka be persuaded, she wondered, once this ordeal was over, to let Ratna find her a man who would give her her due? People said what a sweet child she was, how good-natured and kind, and so she was; she had no reason not to be because she'd always been given whatever she wanted. No one ever said no or denied her. Ratna was only now discovering how strong-willed she was in trying to thwart her. She'd tried to persuade Kanaka to keep the child. What a waste, when the boy was handsome, tall and with fine features, straight limbs and a pleasing manner and the child, if a girl, would surely be a charmer. Once born, the child need not be her burden; all that could be arranged with no one the wiser – Kanaka herself was proof. Nor was she deterred when told that the pain would be severe and not to be taken lightly. Kanaka had remained adamant. Well, they could discuss it again later. The root she'd pounded and made Kanaka swallow was nothing more than amukkara mixed with a little ganja. It would not get rid of the child at all, it had another purpose altogether. Ratna smiled to herself as she thought of how disoriented Kanaka would be when she awakened and felt none of the terrible effects described to her. She'd find her mind emptied by the drug, not her womb. When Ratna returned from telling Nagaveni about Ganapathy, Kanaka would be calm and ready to listen to reason. Nagaveni was wise in the ways of the world. She would know best how to deal with the police, should his body ever be found. She hadn't yet decided whether to tell her mother about Indra. Kanaka at this moment wanted nothing more to do with him, but in a few days she could be made to see differently. Nagaveni could arrange Indra's patronage of Kanaka. Maybe that was the easiest solution. Or maybe now was the time for Ratna to act in her own best interests.

Seeing that Kanaka was deep asleep, Ratna carefully extricated herself, transferring the girl's head from her lap to a pillow. She shook out the girl's dhavani, which had come loose, and covered her with the thin cotton. Then Ratna returned to the parcel Kanaka had brought with her, containing, she'd said, the jewels the boy Indra had given her, and carried it over to her dressing table. It was heavy for its size, and jingled. She opened the knot and unfolded its four corners. Each separate jewel lay wrapped in muslin. She carefully uncovered one, then another, cooing with delight at each new revelation. Not that Ratna had no jewels of her own. It was a matter of pride with Vallabendran, a marker of his caste and status as the raja, to always be generous, ostentatiously so, and over the fourteen years of their relationship he'd marked every festival and ceremonial occasion with a gift worthy of her position as his favoured mistress. But precious as those marks of his regard undoubtedly were, they were not like these pieces. Hers could be bought from any reputable goldsmith in any of the nearby big towns. These were ornaments of a workmanship so fine and set with gemstones of a quality so perfect in colour and cut that she had never before seen their like. Even Devayani had no such jewels. A band of gold in a pattern of leaping fish fitted neatly around her wrist by a hinged opening, held closed with a golden pin. There were bangles both thin and wide, and chains, and rings, one with an emerald as big as her fingernail, and even gold toe rings, for royalty, unlike other castes, were allowed to wear that precious metal anywhere, even below the waist. She weighed in her hands the gold anklets with their myriad tiny bells, and smiled, remembering that the jingling was meant to wake a wary mother-in-law should the pretty girl who wore them try to sneak out to meet her lover. Sighing almost as if in pain, Ratna held up a hair ornament like a lotus, with tear-shaped rubies for petals. She bent towards the mirror and fixed the hook in her hair, letting the flower dangle so that it bloomed in the centre of her forehead. Another, like a crescent moon, shaped of sapphires increasing in size to the centre then decreasing, she pinned to one side, and to the other, a full moon paved with citrons. She unscrewed her own earrings and replaced them with emerald studs to which were attached golden jimikis like hanging rosebuds with stamens of seed pearls. A diamond set in an intricate raised design flashed with a rare brilliance in a nose pin. She twisted her own diamond out and this one in, turning her head this way and that to admire how perfectly its size and shape nestled in the curve of her shapely, chiselled nose, shooting out rays with each movement. Against her dark skin, the diamond flashed like lightning in a rain cloud. No wonder no one questioned the veracity of Nagaveni's story, for who would believe she and Kanaka were not sisters, one dawn, one dusk?

Then, as the tasks that needed doing impinged on her mind, she again became matter-of-fact and impatient, going to the window and pushing open the shutters. Soon the sky would lighten. Parakeets already shrieked and quarrelled over the green berries of the neem tree outside. Ratna needed to reach the village before the first puja and Kanaka's absence was noticed. She would talk to Nagaveni slyly, not revealing everything she knew. Then she, Ratna, could decide what should be their best course of action. She quickly packed the jewels away again and slipped the packet underneath the pillow on which Kanaka lay. At this movement the girl gave a low moan, but did not open her eyes or stir.

Ratna repleated her sari, shaking the folds straight and tucking them before throwing the pallav over her shoulder and pulling the fabric tight to outline her breasts in the short tight bodice that only courtesans and low-caste women wore. Thank god she wasn't a Brahmin who'd have to let her breasts sag, unfettered, covered only by the sari's fabric. Once again she bent over the sleeping girl, decided she was sleeping soundly and nudged the swing so it rocked like a cradle before going out. She closed the blue painted door and as she was about to latch it, she noticed the items in the lamp niche just beside it – the false braid and the hairpins, earrings and glass bangles. She gathered up these things in her two hands and dumped them inside, leaving the mess for the maid to tidy. So Janardana had come back from his night-time adventures while she'd been talking with Kanaka, and desirous not to be seen, had undressed here. The cloth that he'd tied to mark him as a woman would have been retied to return him to manhood. Ratna wondered what he'd overheard, and what he'd put together. Should it give her cause to worry? She had been loyal to him, keeping his secret, but would he be as loyal to her, if he knew his family honour was involved? Surely he couldn't have heard much with the windows and door closed. She and Kanaka had spoken in hushed voices even without thought of a listener, for the matters they'd discussed were ones that naturally induced caution. And the girl hadn't used a name but had relied on circumlocutions, hadn't she? It was customary to avoid speaking the name of the man who stood in that relationship to her. She tried to recall Kanaka's exact words, but they had been so disjointed that it had taken Ratna, hearing all of them, many leaps of understanding to finally make sense of the events she described.

Kanaka hadn't started at the beginning, if the story could even be said to have one, but with the end, with the waiting and watching for the dark-skinned boy with the long curls, who'd spoken such words of love, but who never came. She'd started to cry then, in reliving her fear and desolation, so the story of why she had been desperate for him to meet her that particular night came out in muffled sobs. 'Ganapathy must have seen me when I left the temple garden, and then followed the path I'd made in walking back and forth to the tank. He might even have watched us making love. He knew that the generous boy gave me jewels, but he wanted both, the gold and to have me as well. I should have kept quiet, let that bastard take whatever he wanted, but I couldn't bear the touch of his hard, calloused hands, not then, not right after *his* caresses.' 'You certainly could have handled it better. You should know by now how to deal with men who want to take a bite of the fruit that someone else has paid for.' 'It was Durga. She understood only that he was hurting me. Isn't it true that there are secret places on the body where if you press with the right amount of force, it will kill a man? The varma adi practitioners, who heal by pressing on certain points while hiding their hands under a blanket, say so. It must have been like that; for suddenly the arm that held me so I couldn't move fell away, and he sat down, *dhoom*, as if struck, with that look on his face of surprise. He'd felt no pain, I think, just the sudden weakness. There was the hair ornament, sticking out of his thigh. It is so slender, not even as thick as my little finger, and where it entered, just that one drop of blood. Durga had pushed it all the way in. We both stared at it, he and I, while Durga ran away, saying, "Kanaka, Kanaka, Kanaka." How happy it would have made me at any other time, hearing her speak my name. Then he reached out himself with trembling fingers, grasped the little parakeet somehow, for his hand seemed hardly in his control, and drew it out very slowly from his flesh. I suppose he must have thought it was like a thorn that had somehow caused the sapping of all his strength. That is when the blood spurted out and didn't stop. It streamed between his legs and soaked into the earth. I could only watch in horror as his twitching ceased and his eyes glazed over with the look of death.'

Ratna thought to herself, 'What a waste of a good drummer. They are hard to come by.' She had not been spared Ganapathy's attentions, of course, but she'd been older and her heart had not been given to another. She could not have kept Vallabendran's interest in her for fourteen years without sometimes finding her own satisfaction elsewhere.

And only then did Kanaka come to the part Ratna had already surmised must be at the start somewhere, the secret lovemaking at the old tank, carried on by the flimsy subterfuge of the false name. 'Chee! What a thin and transparent lie! As if there are two girls matching your description in this place. Anyone might have told him who you are supposed to be to him and, of course, that would be the end of it. You said it yourself, he's not like others, who have no qualms about fucking their daughters, much less their sisters. You should have told him the facts, made it clear to him that it's all just a story meant to keep you safe from that lecher, my fine and noble patron, his father.'

'He spoke such sweet words that I trembled inside to hear them. He said we should marry, so I could ride with him in his car, and walk with him along Marina beach in Madras, as the white people do, arm in arm. I thought a boy with fine ideas like that would not be so easily swayed by what someone else might tell him.'

'No one ever goes there any more, since the tank dried up. The two of you carried on long enough without anyone seeing. So the body may never be found.'

'And maybe it will be found tomorrow.'

'Even if it is, why should anyone point to you as the one responsible? A jealous husband is more likely. Shouldn't we just leave it to fate?'

'Would you say that if I was sick? No, you'd go to the siddhar and get some medicine. We don't just wait and hope that our troubles will be solved by destiny.'

'Yes, we ask for help, from those who can help us.'

'I asked for help, from him! But he never came. Now I must find my own way out of this mess.'

'Maybe he didn't get your note.'

'The maidservant swore she put it into his hand.'

'That hair ornament, had anyone seen you wear it?'

'Everyone. Subbu, for one.'

'That boy would die for you, so you can be sure he'd lie.'

'What lie could he tell? It's a courtesan's ornament, not the kind of thing married women wear. And no one except one of us has the thick hair to hold a hairpin so heavy. Someone would be sure to point that out, Ganapathy's wife, if no one else.'

'Well, it could have been any one of us then, me, or Nagaveni.'

'Exactly. Don't you see? If I stay here, one of us will pay the price, whichever one they choose, for the police will have to declare someone responsible, otherwise what are they good for? But if I'm nowhere to be found, they can safely make me the culprit.'

'Yes, I suppose if we give them the right incentives they can be convinced to look no further. Oh, why couldn't you have hidden the body better? Or at least pried the pin from his fingers?'

'I didn't think. All I wanted was to get away as quickly as possible. Anyway, I couldn't have touched him. You would understand if you'd watched him die.'

'But really, are you sure you have to go away? Sometimes a secret is revealed by the very act of trying to conceal it.'

'If I stayed I would have to eat my food as if nothing was wrong, braid my hair and dress myself as if nothing was wrong, go on living as if nothing terrible had happened. I'm not able to do that. I thought he loved me more, with all that honey that poured from his lips, but it turns out I love him more, for never having spoken of it.'

Ratna had defended Indra, saying, 'You should have told him yourself what your relationship is supposed to be. Admit your mistake in this.'

'It isn't true, so why even bring it up? How could he think that of me, that I would give myself to him like that?'

'Let me set the matter right. He might not believe anyone else, but he'd have to believe me, the one who bore you.'

'No, it's too late. Our love grew in the spring, and now in the heat it has shrivelled up.'

'What's your plan then?'

'I don't know. Let me be rid of the child, then I'll think about it.'

'Well, I'm happy you got the better of Vallabendran. He won't want you now that Indra's had you.'

'Won't he be angry?'

'Of course. His pride will be hurt. But he'll see I had no part in it, and he'll come to me to be consoled.'

Ratna walked through her well-tended garden, blooming with jasmine that in the summer heat released their sweet perfume. The frangipani tree, bare of leaves, was full of buds. In a day or two they would unfurl. The gate proclaimed her house to be Madangriha – House of Love's Intoxication. As she opened the gate she noticed that the scrub grass around the gatepost was covered in small orange-capped mushrooms. This was a bad omen, a sure sign of malevolent forces at work against her. Perhaps this accounted for the waning of Vallabendran's affections, which she'd felt for many months now. More worrying than his inability to perform was his lack of desire itself, so that his impotence seemed only the symptom of some more insidious disease. She had taken all the recommended precautions in consultation with the wild woman who made potions and cast spells, trying out in secret various magical means to win back his love, as well as cooking and feeding him the aphrodisiacs that were supposed to be most efficacious, lotus root, mutton, jackfruit seeds. But the situation hadn't improved: either Vallabendran had simply tired of her or something caused him to be tired.

Ratna had said to the girl, without really meaning it, 'Maybe we can go together to Madras.' Now the orange mushrooms seemed to signal that it was time for her to quit this place altogether. In Georgetown, she'd heard, artists of great repute lived in grand style and found rich and influential patrons among the Chettiar merchants and Brahmin agents and translators for the British. They could establish themselves there with new antecedents, using Indra's jewels as surety. Kanaka could dance, there was no doubt about that, and Ratna could sing. Many girls from villages like Pandanallur and Kumbakonam with far more dubious credentials and not half as pretty were making names for themselves in Madras. She wouldn't tell Nagaveni everything, this idea she'd keep to herself.

Immersed in these thoughts, she came to the two tamarind trees growing close together right in the middle of the path. Anyone who didn't know, and looked from the main road, would think that it led only here, to this shaded refuge, for her house was completely hidden behind the two massive trunks. It was only as she skirted the trees that she saw Vallabendran approaching along the main road on horseback. Ratna cursed under her breath. His coming on her so suddenly amplified the feeling that unseen forces were at work. Something had distracted her, not just worries and daydreams, but the malign influence that had exerted its power over the girl for the whole day and night and had now extended its field to include her. She should have heard the hoofbeats, should have hidden herself until he had gone on ahead towards his own house, as she felt he had fully intended to do. But it was too late, he had seen her, and seen that she had seen him.

He turned his horse on to the path as she stood and waited. When he reached her, she greeted him with proper deference and respect. 'My lord. After all these years, you can still surprise me. You find me unprepared, for this is not the time you usually choose to honour me with your presence.' 'Nor is it usual for you to be setting out so early.' He remained on the horse, which shook its head with impatience. She realized he was very tired. Ratna didn't know if his impotence was a condition that bothered him only with her, or if the fear of it kept him from other women too, common prostitutes, or the wives of men who worked for him. She couldn't ask, since they both pretended no such problem existed. So she said with a hint of jealousy, to flatter his ego, 'Someone's been keeping you awake the whole night.' 'Your eyes are bloodshot too, I see,' he replied. 'Didn't you say to me, "Your body is my body," and now it's come true. You've made love the whole night, and I'm the one who shows the effects.' It was the kind of pretty conceit that used to amuse and charm him into a better mood, but this time Vallabendran's scowl seemed to harden. He dismounted in one quick movement and letting go of the horse's reins, grabbed Ratna by the chin, turning her face and examining it. 'Where were you going so early in the morning? No lies, the simple truth.' 'To the midwife. I have a pain,' Ratna said, realizing as the words came out of her mouth that he could misconstrue them in his anger. 'Perhaps there is another reason you need her services?' 'No.' 'No? Who gave you this nose ring?' The question took Ratna completely by surprise, and her fingers flew up to feel the jewel. Only then did she realize he was referring to the one she'd forgotten to remove. 'Janardana gave it to me,' she said, saying the first name that came to mind. 'What business of his is it to give you gifts?' 'It was a small token, in return for . . . keeping a secret.' 'Liar. Small? One thing you and your kind know is the value of gems. Diamonds of this water aren't plucked from trees.' Ratna backed away from him, weeping. With tears she could usually bring him around. 'Yes, clench your fists. Do you want to hit me?' Vallabendran said, 'Shut up. Did you think I wouldn't recognize my own mother's nose pin? Tell me who gave it to you.' Ratna struggled free of him and stepped back further. Her fingers went to the jewel and for a moment it seemed as if she was going to untwist it from the small hole. But then she dropped her hands and stood facing him. 'No, I won't give it to you. It was a gift given in a moment of love, and even the one who gave it can't ask for it back.' 'No one has a right to that jewel except me.' He covered the distance between them in two long steps. Ratna turned and tried to run, but Vallabendran caught her by the braid and pulled her so hard she had to stop. 'My lord! You're hurting me.' 'Yes.' One hand still held her by the rope of her hair, while the other slid down and grasped the tapering end with the braided tassel. He twisted it around her neck and pulled it tight. 'Who gave you the jewel? No lies this time.'

Ratna's eyes widened in fear as he pushed her hard against the tree. She clawed at the braid and tried to take a breath. By turning her head, she was able to loosen it slightly and say, 'It wasn't stolen.' Vallabendran jerked her head back and pulled the two ends tighter. 'Tell me the name.' Ratna swayed, almost falling, her cheek against the rough bark, but his grip on her braid forced her to stay upright. 'I can't breathe,' she mouthed, but hardly any sound came out. Vallabendran loosened his grip slightly and Ratna choked and coughed with the sudden intake of breath. 'Out with it! I want the name.' 'Please, my lord. I can explain . . .' 'The name. All I want is the name.' And she felt the bite of the braid into her neck again. She tried to tell him about Kanaka and his son, but her mouth was being pressed into the tree and she couldn't properly form the words. 'Indra,' she managed to say. Vallabendran roared, 'You whore!' and pulled the braid tighter and tighter. There was so much she wanted to tell him, and in her mind she found the words, but he would never hear them. 'When you leave, my lord, I worship your back and when you come back, I worship your front, so whichever side you show me is as good as the other. If you fit me like a sword fits the scabbard, my lord, it is because I've made myself in the image of your desires. I like what you like, my lord, and take only what you're itching to give. If you want me on top, then on top I get. If you want to fuck my pox-ridden maid, then don't I bring her to you in my own bed? When you've had enough, then that's when we stop. You were my mother's lover, until Nagaveni said, "He's a hard nut," and turned you over to me. You thought you were the first, but no, a virgin is not like an egg, that you can tell when it's cracked. My virginity which you paid so much for was just a trick I practised with Pasupati.' She could feel Vallabendran's arms shaking with the effort of pulling her braid and hear the sharp rasp of his breath in her ear, but she had left his grasp. She was back in the room with the priest. What a child she'd been then, turning her face away from his greedy mouth, pressing her thighs together, squeezing shut her eyes. She was sure he'd split her open and she'd howled and screamed. Only when he'd spilt his seed and fallen away from her, breathing heavily, one leg still weighing her down, had she opened her eyes. The world had shifted and yet it looked exactly the same. After some time the priest had again tied his cloth and left, but she'd lain still, unable to sleep, staring at the ceiling. Yes, it was above her, but to the lizard chasing a moth, it was underneath. And then the next morning at the puja she'd called him out of habit by the old name, 'Anna – older brother', and he'd turned and for a moment their eyes had met. She'd seen his shame just as he must have seen her revulsion. And yet he came back each night. What Nagaveni had said as she'd pushed Ratna into the room with him and bolted the door turned out to be true, 'The thorniest path becomes easier each time it is trod.' The next night, she'd sobbed more quietly, and the night after that she'd lain still and let him do as he liked. It was better not to struggle. Her legs weakened and it was only the pressure of Vallabendran's body pressing her against the tree that kept her upright. With a last effort, she clutched with her hands at the braid. But she could only reach the bottu, the symbol of her marriage to the great god. That was what she pulled at as she slid to the base of the tree, until finally the string broke and the black beads flew everywhere.

The Sorceress

My mother-in-law never tired of cursing me, 'With your unlucky face, why did I marry you to my son? It was a big mistake. All you have learned is to eat. You are getting strong as a buffalo and just as dark, with a backside like an elephant.' She complained about me no matter how little I ate. Nothing but rice gruel with salt and a few chillies in the morning. And in the evening I got accustomed to suppressing my hunger. No matter what time it was, I could eat only after they had all eaten, and that too whatever little was left over. Afraid of his mother's scolding, my husband ate heartily in case she accused him of going hungry in order to leave something more for me.

And if I failed to pay her respect, she said, 'Look how you treat me. No wonder the rains have failed.' In one human being, the water that comes from the eyes, the nose, the mouth, the skin, the bladder, is different. So is it any surprise that human beings in the same way differ in name, quality and quantity?

I was happy whenever my mother-in-law said, 'Go and fetch water.' Any excuse to leave the house. Because we eat even squirrels and crabs and take away the dead bodies of cows, the people of the village despise us, and do not let us draw water from any well. I had to walk a long way to fetch water. Women of my caste are not allowed to carry the pot on our hips, and with the pot on my head, the sway of my hips was not easy to ignore. I was strong. I was a good-looking woman. When I walked by, men's glances followed me like schools of fish.

The man in the pukka house called me to him. I wouldn't go. I replied, 'Like a laugh for no reason, love play with a woman without a blouse, dumplings without a filling and a wedding without music, your desire is futile.'

He said, 'That which I can't have will not survive.' The import of his words was clear – he would do some kind of sorcery on me. Each of my children was born healthy and beautiful, but sickened and died. The first one died of a vecca katti, a poisonous tumour, the second of the whooping cough, the third died in my arms of fright. My husband sickened too and wasted away. After that my mother-in-law threw me out and I had no choice but to wander. I sang, 'I'm a woman with no husband or mother-in-law, free of care, I roam the world. I won't bow for the sake of Brahmins, I won't fight for the sake of kings, I won't buy or sell what can't be bought or sold, I'll sing songs for my own pleasure, eat honey and drink the rain.'

One day as I was walking I felt a sharp pain in my foot, as if it had been stabbed with a knife. I looked down but I could see nothing, nothing I stepped on, and no blood, despite the pain. The foot swelled and I began to feel so faint that I lay down at the side of the road and slept. I had a dream in which Mariamman came to me. She said, 'You stepped on my trident, now take it. It will stay with you always.' In the dream she gave me also the pot, the fire and the knife.

After that I could speak with Amma's voice when anyone came to me for help. Sometimes a person faces problems such as they have never seen. Nothing ever goes right, and there is endless suffering. After they consult many people and find no solution, finally they come to me, because only sorcery can cut sorcery. Taking the water with which I wash my menstrual cloths and boiling it until only a thick residue remains, and mixing that with pig's fat I make mai, the powerful compound I use for magic. When people come to me, I give them a small amount of this mai, wrapped in a betel leaf.

In this way, the maid of the devadasi came to me too.

She said, 'Every night I have such bad dreams I'm afraid to sleep. In the day my head aches so I can't enjoy life. Surely a pey has caught me. Give me something to make it leave.'

'When did this begin?'

'I've been suffering for five days like this.'

'Did you go alone to any deserted place, or wander near the burning ground, or journey across some wasteland? Were you going at it in a field somewhere? The odour that comes from bodies rubbing against each other is irresistible to the pey.'

'No, never. I walked to my house and I walked back. I did nothing.'

'Nothing? No one does nothing, and those small somethings add up. What is it you did, this nothing?' At first no one wants to give away their secrets. I had to coax her to tell me. 'She must have a sacrifice if you want her help. Have you seen them, those devotees who pierce their flesh, and give the goddess their own blood to drink? The greatest sacrifice is yourself. Give Mariamman your secret.'

'I didn't kill her! I only threw her body in the well!'

And with that the whole story came out.

'On my way to my mistress's house, I came upon her and the raja fighting. I didn't do anything, because what man bothers to beat a woman if not out of love? And then, when he wouldn't stop, well, what could I do? I'm not her relative.

I kept my mouth shut and stayed perfectly still. But then he turned and saw me. I had no choice but to help him. The master of my mistress is my master too. We put the body on his horse, and I was leading him along the footpath to the house that's kept locked up, where the watchman is always drunk and the well is deep. That's when we saw the pey.'

'You saw it?'

'I didn't know then that's what it was. As we passed by my mistress's house, the two halves of the door opened, the doorway lit by the lamps within so that a figure was silhouetted, one hand on the door frame, one hand clutching her sari. She was as real as real. I saw the glint of bangles on her wrist, I heard the jingle of ankle bells. For a moment I thought it was my mistress herself, but then I remembered and looked – there was her body still, hanging lifeless across the saddle. Suddenly, as if the figure had seen us just as we'd seen her, she banged the door shut and we could see only shadows.

'The raja knew immediately who it was and laughed a terrible laugh. Dropping the reins of the horse, he charged towards the house. "Catch her!" he shouted, and I said, "Yes, lord." He grew in his rage, like a rooster at a cockfight thrusting out its feathers, arching its neck, and I feared for the girl should he catch her. It was as if my mistress had died before he could rid himself of all the emotion she'd aroused, and on seeing the sister, some residue had risen to make him swell and stiffen in anger. I didn't want that wrath turned on me, so I did as I was told. I myself, who know the house and all its nooks and crannies so well, looked under every bed and inside every almirah and chest. We'd seen the door close on her, and all the windows are barred, so had she been human, we'd have surely found her. "Lord," I said, "it is no use to search for a ghost," and he said, "Shut up! Don't talk nonsense. Look again." So we searched one more time, but no girl was to be found anywhere in Ratna's house.'

Silly creature, to pin her belief in the pey on such a foundation. I didn't bother to criticize the parameters of her search. Having seen the lighted doorway and sudden darkness, I would have looked outside for the girl, not inside, for someone can as easily pull the door shut behind when going out as push it closed when staying in. And if I hadn't found her in the garden, I would have looked on the tops of the tall almirahs and in the rafters. We who dabble in magic know that people are quick to search under and in and behind, but rarely look upwards.

'He finally gave up and we returned to our task. When we neared the back gate of the empty house, the raja wrested the jewel from my mistress's nose and, pulling the body off the horse, mounted himself and rode off, leaving her in a heap at my feet. I had to drag her the rest of the way to the well. So what if I took her brocade blouse and the sari?'

'You must not keep anything she was wearing when she died. You may give them to me. Go and fetch a cockerel for the exorcism, and I will make all the other preparations.'

I called the parai drummer, made a whisk of neem branches, impaled limes on each prong of my trident, found a stone as big as a head. I drew a circle on the ground and placed the woman at its centre facing east, so when the pey left her body it would be contained until I could trap it. As the drum beat out the trance-inducing rhythm, I sang to the pey, 'Tell me your good name, you are now free to speak. Dance and sing out your name!' Lighting camphor on a plate, I waved it in front of her. It caught her gaze and she stared, beginning to jerk and sway in the movement of trance. I squeezed the juice of the limes all over her face, for that is the essence of the goddess and frightens the pey into speaking. I whipped her with the leafy neem whisk, as Mariamman had fanned herself to keep the flies from her open oozing sores, while I called, 'Tell me which lock of hair now holds you!' and when she showed me, I tied it into a knot. 'Come out, come out, I'll give you a life for the one you're leaving.' I bit off the head of the cockerel and poured the blood from its neck into her mouth. She spat it out and the pey shrieked. I thrust the stone into her hands, and she ran with it this way and that while I followed. When finally she dropped the stone and fell senseless to the ground, I cut the lock of hair with the pey in it, and nailed it to the tamarind tree.

When she became herself again, I gave her the mai, saying, 'Rub this on each threshold and window of your house. She won't enter after that, and you'll be left in peace. Now walk home without once looking back over your shoulder.'

I did not tell the maid what I had seen. It must have been later the same morning they'd searched for the girl and hadn't found her. Through a curtain of leaves, as the light came up, I saw my goddess in the form of a slender young maiden perched high in the branches of a tree in the compound of the devadasi's house. I gazed upwards in awe at her beauty, her skin the same reddish gold of the tender sprouting leaves of the mango tree in the rosy light of dawn. I sang words in her praise, 'Oh ever-changing Mother, Mother like rain, who becomes a jewel through my chants, you are flames, you are embers, I burn as I gaze upon you, destroy my ills, let your mercy grow until the whole world is saved, oh pretty one, stay with me who worship you.' I wasn't surprised because my goddess appears to me in many forms, sometimes wonderful, sometimes fearsome. I went on my way, singing, and when I returned by the same path, she was gone.

The Priest

Listen to the rain, so loud and unrelenting. There, the distant rumble of thunder, the sky god angry at stubbing his toe and muttering, we say. Your sari will be soaked in the time it takes to run from here to the car. Stay. Let the driver sleep. No one will come at this time and we will be undisturbed. There is more to the story that has made our little temple famous. Do you want to see the golden image for yourself, or do you want to beg the same god who granted that boon to grant you another? All of us who worship here have our troubles. You are no different.

The temple is not a building like a house or a school or a factory, though those too must follow the laws of vaasthu or there will never be any success. The temple is the universe. It is also the body of the deity, Shiva's body. There is no contradiction, because the cosmos is nothing other than Shiva's body.

When in their love games his consort Parvathi playfully covered Shiva's eyes for just a moment, the whole world was plunged into darkness. A drop of sweat on the god's forehead, heated by passion and touched by the beautiful lotus-petal hands of the goddess, grew from an embryo into a being, blind, deformed and hungry enough to eat up the whole world. This son of Shiva was at the same time a demon, so eventually he needed to be defeated. By then his great power enveloped all of existence, requiring all the gods to unite to defeat him. Together they pressed him face down and splayed into the ground, each god pinning down one part of his body. This is Vaasthu Devata, who resides in any place having four walls and to whom offerings must be made. He wakes up for some time on eight days of the year, which are the auspicious times to begin construction.

The foundation of the sanctum is the earth and takes up the space from the god's feet to his knees. The walls made of stone, two feet thick, solid as they seem, are water and form the god from his knees to his loins. The vimana, which rises above the roof elaborately carved, is vivid flame, and takes us from his loins to his heart. The kaalasa, the finial pot, is air and goes from his heart to the meeting of his eyebrows. The pointed needle on top of the pot is akasa, ether, and goes from his eyebrows to the top of his head. So wherever you are in the temple you are in him or on him.

Turn away from the smell of the rain, to the smell of the black stone. The way to the sanctum sanctorum is completely covered, dark and cool, with bats hanging above us in the corners. The walls are impregnated with the smoke of sambrani waved before the deity, the inky unguent called krsnaghanda rubbed to make him glossy black, the scent of tuberose and marigold in garlands brought by women with jasmine threaded in their black, oiled hair. When I was the priest this is where I did my work, immersed in these smells. Now I am supposed to stay far away, to see him only from a distance, if I can glimpse him at all. I had to find a way to get close enough once more to this intoxication.

Near the sanctum the carving is simple and refined so that all the devotee's attention can go towards the god.

The sanctum is the womb house, pregnant with the deity. The construction is done only after the ground, chosen for its auspiciousness and oriented towards the south-west, is sanctified by rituals. A pure copper pot filled with nine kinds of gems and efficacious herbs is buried in the centre. The icon is installed over this, the pitha or seat, facing east.

Our great god Maheshwara appears in the temple in the form of a linga, so you might say he is manifested, since he is visible before us, but he is also unmanifested, because he appears as a purely geometric shape, without revealing any of his attributes. The visible linga is not the proper object of worship but the support for the devotee, standing in front of the open door to the sanctum with hands pressed together and eyes raised, who sees his true form only with the mind's eye. As the devotee looks at the deity, the deity looks back, because the god's eyes have been opened in the ceremony of 'opening the eyes' where, using a chisel of gold and a hammer of silver, the sthapati opens first the right eye and then the left, and all organs of sense and all orifices. The god is then shown what is very auspicious first – the vulva of a cow with her calf, green paddy sprouts, a virgin girl, a married woman, nine types of grains, and so on, with a black cloth quickly placed in between so that nothing inauspicious enters the god's line of vision by mistake.

When the first signs of this disease appeared on my body, I took that gold coin I'd kept so long and never before had reason to spend to the great Vira Bhadra Sthapati of Swamimalai, saying, 'Make a beautiful lamp for me, which I can give to whichever god cures me of this disease.'

The measurements for the carving in wax, which must be perfect to the most minute and intricate detail, are made according to this schema: eight particles is equal to one breadth of a thread; eight breadths of a thread are equal to one breadth of the hair from a horse's tail; eight hairs from a horse's tail are equal to one grain of sand; eight grains of sand are equal to one mustard seed; eight mustard seeds are equal to one bamboo seed. The measurement is based on proportions, not absolutes. The sthapati chooses a ribbon of palm leaf of the length the finished object should be. He folds it in two, and in two again and again to get his markings in the proportion of two, four, eight, sixteen, thirty-two and sixty-four. Using these markings, he fixes the exact dimension of each part of the image – the length of the forehead is four divisions, from eyebrow to chin is thirteen and a half, the neck is four and the thigh, from pubis to knee, is twenty-seven. Until the image is finished, the ribbon of palm leaf is kept soft and pliant in a bowl of water. Moreover, each part is shaped according to a metaphor that comes from the poet: brow like a bow, lower lip like a tinda fruit, knee like a crab. The sthapati allows the image to emerge out of his thoughts on these objects as he sits in a meditative state. As he carves and sculpts the wax, he remembers stories, legends, poems, dreams. Wherever the proportions are correct, there is harmony between the five primary elements of the universe.

He meditated on the form, sculpted it, perfect in every detail, in wax, made a mould from clay, heated the clay so the wax image was lost, melting away, so no other lamp could be made exactly like the one he made for me. He poured the molten bell metal bright as gold into the mould, chiselled and polished every detail of jewellery and dress. When he gave me the finished object, I was amazed. He'd made the lamp as a devadasi, a girl with a long braid, slightly out-thrust hip and hands cupped together in front in pushpanjali hasta, ready to attend to the god.

I carried the image with me to the Vaithiswara temple in Maiyiladurai, where Shiva cured Angaragan of leprosy, and Ettumarai, where the priests gave me medicated ghee and the blackened oil from the temple lamp at the entrance for forty-one days, and the Shatabdi Pattaleswara temple, where Shiva cures skin diseases, and the Dhanwantari temple in Thottuva, where a man was cured of leprosy after staying there for forty-one days and bathing in the stream. I crawled on my belly from the beach to Arthungal Church and offered my obeisance to St Stephen and drank the water from the well at St George's Church at Edathua. A Mussalman sitting behind the Beemapally mosque made cuts all over my body to let the bad blood while saying, 'Oh Allah! The Sustainer of Mankind! Remove the illness, cure the disease.' I carried the lamp with me from place to place, but despite all my wandering, I never found any god or goddess in church or mosque or temple who could relieve my suffering. I grew tired of wandering and wanted to return here to the god I knew best. When the disease had so progressed that no one would recognize me, I traced the journey back. But I knew I could not be satisfied only to sit and beg the whole day long in the entranceway of the temple and never come close to the deity I used to serve so intimately.

With the few pice that I collect, I buy what food I can and eat when the priest, my brother-in-law, locks the great outer door and leaves for the home that used to be mine. I stumble down to the river on my stumps of feet in the dusk and bathe when no one else is there. Then, instead of going back along the path to the village, I join the unused track between the old tank and the gate on the back wall of the temple garden.

From the temple garden, I can make my way unseen to the man-sized door cut into the west-facing gate where the great wooden temple car rests. In my grandfather's or maybe my great-grandfather's time, it was said that the car wouldn't move no matter how many men pulled it unless a human being was sacrificed in its path, and so it was done, and dragged through the streets each year. But ever since the British outlawed the custom, it has stood immovable. It is easy enough to enter the temple by this unused door, but no one would dare. I am committing no crime, as others would fear to do. I know the Agamas, and what they say is that I do not lose my caste rights for my condition. I enter only to perform my own worship.

Every evening I take the lamp from its hiding place and make my offering of flowers, leaves and light, first in front of the great god, then to his consort, then to Rahu at the auspicious time as I have calculated it. When I am finished, I tidy everything away, and go to sleep under the temple car, next to the stack of thick wooden poles that carry the palanquins for the deities. I make sure to be gone the way I came in before the first puja, leaving no sign of my ever having been there.

One night as I made my way from the river to the back gate of the temple garden, I heard the sounds of wild pigs before I came upon them in the dusk. There must have been six at least. They scattered at my presence, and I saw for a moment what they'd been gobbling – a man's naked torso, the entrails pulled out and spread on the ground – before they grouped again around it and, ignoring me, went back to feasting. I hurried away as fast as I could. It was no business of mine, but the sight had shocked me.

Even after I'd performed the pujas, and lain down between the great wooden wheels of the temple car, I couldn't sleep. If I closed my eyes, I saw the bloodied snouts of the pigs, I heard their grunts and the tearing of flesh. I kept my eyes open, waiting for the night to end. Thus, when the hinges of the great door creaked, I heard the sound. I crawled deeper into the shadows and sat up, listening and waiting, fearing some further horror. The night sounds of buzzing insects drowned out my own furtive thoughts, the beat of my heart like a drum. To calm myself, I repeated the mantra to Garuda my father had taught me, for protection from dark forces. At the seventh repetition, a figure appeared coming directly towards my hiding place, slender, silent and dark as a shadow. I knew immediately who it was, by the grace of her walk. I thought I had been discovered, but no, Kanaka kept going past the car. I crawled to the other side and listened from the deepest shadows as she climbed on to one of the palanquins. I heard the slide of metal against metal, the twisting of a screw and a faint jingle muffled by cloth. She jumped down, and disappeared the way she'd come, and after a few moments I heard the creak of the great door closing.

I wanted to see what Kanaka did next, so I made my way to the main entrance. I found it locked as it should be, so to leave the temple I had no choice but to exit as I had entered, by the west gate. The thin sliver of new moon was tangled in the branches of jungle trees, like a silver chain snagged in some girl's net of dark curls.

There was no sign of the girl so I walked towards the main road, seeing no one, hearing no untoward sound. I'd reached the boundary of the village, where the clay horses and warriors guard us from those who could cause harm, and was ready to turn back when I saw her in the shadows, sitting on the stone marker, tense, expectant. I was near her, very near, and all that kept her from seeing me was that she faced away, and it was so very dark. I moved slowly and silently back behind a tree and waited to discover what it was she was waiting for.

Forgive me for telling you things you already know, but they are mixed up with things of which you have no knowledge, so I can't give you one without the other.

She waited restlessly, rising, taking a few steps to peer into the darkness before returning to sit again. Once or twice she seemed almost ready to give up. When the moon like the sharpened edge of a scythe had reached its highest point in the sky, she'd even taken some steps in the direction from which she'd come, passing by where I hid, as if returning home. But like an ant clinging to a leaf in a stream, even as it's being dragged into a vortex, she seemed unable to let go of the hope to which she clung against all evidence. But when almost imperceptibly the sky began to lighten, she turned and walked away without looking back. I watched her go. I thought, 'She came to meet her lover and he didn't turn up, exactly as it happens in the padams she dances. Now she will go home.'

I went back to the temple.

Remember I listed the many ways to tell a story, river's flow, lion's glance, frog's hop and flower garland? I have used all these devices to hold your interest. But now I must use the mode most fittingly used at the end, where I come directly, swiftly and precisely to the point, like a raptor sighting its prey, falcon's dive.

Once inside the temple I lit one of the lamps and carried it with me to check what Kanaka had been doing in the dark corner near my secret bed. Holding up the lamp, I saw that she'd removed the brass cap and pin covering the hole on the palanquin where the processional deity would be fixed on it. It was a clever hiding place, since only in preparation for the particular festival days when the god was taken in procession would anyone disturb these objects. I thought about what she might have hidden there, something fitting within that small cavity that, though wrapped in cloth, jingled. I wondered why at this time she'd taken it.

Nothing else seemed out of place, until nearing the sanctum, I heard a voice repeating Ka na ka Ka na ka like a mantra. In one dark corner of the colonnade of circumambulation around the sanctum, I could barely see the reflection of the flickering flame in a pair of dark eyes. It was the little girl Durga, staring as if in a trance. I said in an urgent whisper, 'Durga! Durga! Come out!' but she said nothing, nor did she seem by any sign to have heard me. Her eyes were fixed, like those of the carved figures on the wall beside her. As I held the lamp closer, I saw that her hands were tied to the pillar with a strip of cloth torn from a dhavani.

Until I saw the child, I thought that at any moment Kanaka would enter to carry out her usual tasks, to prepare the flowers, the ritual objects, the camphor. Soon after that my brother-in-law and Subbu would follow, to awaken the god.

But Kanaka wouldn't have restrained her in this way if she had any intention of coming back. Why would she bother? Poor Durga. Usually the child would sit wherever Kanaka put her, indifferent to time or place. But if noise, or the tumult of many people frightened her, she would seek a dark corner to hide, and wouldn't come out until pulled out. Kanaka would only have tied Durga to make sure she was found, when Kanaka herself wasn't around to care for her. I put down the lamp, and struggled to untie the knot that held her with my stiff and misshapen hands. She shrank from my touch and as soon as the cloth loosened, in one swift movement she yanked it from my hand and ran. Later, I would have to make sure that someone found her.

So it was no surprise to me when Kanaka did not arrive as she should have. While my brother-in-law sent Subbu to the devadasi quarter to fetch her, I had plenty of time to ponder. The dead body in the jungle between the back gate of the temple garden and the old tank. The cloth bag containing something that jingled hidden in the procession palanquin. The girl waiting on the boundary stone for someone who never came. Even if I didn't understand everything, I understood in a flash that Kanaka was in trouble, that she'd run away and wasn't coming back.

In those days when I was trying to cure my disease by worshipping one god after another, I took part in a ritual for the goddess that the low-caste people worship, the black, powerful Mariamman, who commands and controls the forces that bring disease. In front of the boundary stones of the village the pariahs take a pig, cut it down the middle and place it so its blood soaks into a pile of cooked rice. The priest mixes the blood and rice into a ball and holds it at the pig's mouth. If the pig eats it, the sacrifice can proceed. The priest makes more balls of pig's blood and rice, and walking to each boundary stone of the village, with the drums beating and the crowds chanting and dancing in frenzy, he throws a ball of rice up into the air and catches it, once, twice. On the third time it goes up into the air, but doesn't come back down. This is the sign the goddess has accepted and all will be well. The action is repeated at each corner of the village, each time with the goddess accepting her gift. The village will be safe and the pig can be cooked and eaten. The miracle is achieved by a trick so simple that it could fool no one, or so you think. The third time, after having really thrown and caught it twice, the priest merely makes the action of throwing. Our eyes follow the trajectory, seeing the ball, seeing it disappear. But it hasn't been thrown up at all. The priest has simply, smoothly, quickly in the same movement passed it into his empty hand and into the pot.

That is how the idea came to me. I saw the way in which a pattern could be made that drew attention to some curves and lines and obscured others, making a design with figure and ground. Out of the accidents of my life and your life, the leap could be made, from 18 to 108. That is what others would see, while we kept the bitter truth to ourselves.

I took the beautiful lamp cast in the form of a devadasi by Vira Bhadra Sthapati from its hiding place. Where did I hide it, you ask? With all the other lamps and ritual objects in the storeroom. When my lamp stood as one among more than twenty, neither Kanaka, nor my brother-in-law nor Subbu had even noticed it. I positioned the image of bell metal carefully in the sanctum, knowing how it would shine when caught in the circular path of the lighted camphor, then closed the door and stood quietly in the darkest corner. I covered my head as best I could with my upper cloth, keeping my feet hidden by the dhoti, and my arms crossed so my hands couldn't be seen. Standing behind the small crowd of worshippers, when the light from the camphor lit the small golden figure, I said, 'Kanaka.'

You must be tired of listening, since so much is your own story with no need of my telling. But I wanted to lay my part at your feet, and now I have done so.

You should go, before Subbu sees you. He is now the priest of the temple, keeping alive our family connection with this sacred spot. He does all the daily rituals in the prescribed manner, but his attention, as he waves the brass plate with the camphor in front of the devotee, is elsewhere. He tries to be a Brahmin without being brahminical, just as I try to have leprosy without being a leper, but it is a difficult inversion to practise. I thought of revealing myself to him, since I could see how much he was suffering, but I've held myself back. His intimate connection to a person with my disease would cause him great conflict. Should he try to ignore me completely as he went about his duties, with his own disfigurement, or should he acknowledge me and suffer the loss of standing and prestige? I didn't want to put him to that test.

And if Subbu came to know, so would my wife. The laws of Manu as regards her duty demand that she take care of me no matter how disgusting my condition. Lepers being taken care of by faithful Indian wives is a popular type of story. How could I subject Brhadambal to that? Even with no husband around, no one dare say she's that most inauspicious thing, a widow. She still wears the kumkum in the parting of her hair, and does the puja daily and fasts for the well-being of a husband she remembers as an honourable man, of impeccable morals, handsome, strong and wise. Why should I tell her he no longer exists?

Ratna's house is now occupied by the girl who used to be the maidservant. She lives there as if she were the mistress herself, even dressing in the silk saris and the jewels Ratna left behind. Nagaveni tried her best to claim those things for herself but when she appealed to Vallabendran, he sided with the maid, letting her keep everything, it is said, except a diamond nose pin worth more than a house. She's no beauty, but she must have picked up some skills from Ratna for she's never without a man.

Though devadasis are no longer allowed to take part in the temple ritual, Nagaveni still lives in the house that goes with the performance of such duties. She still leads a troupe of musicians and dancers, travelling with them to perform in towns and villages all around. She wields the cymbals herself, because the old nattuvanar moved to Madras, and she's got herself a new young drummer because Ganapathy never returned. Nagaveni supports his family in spite of his wife's insults and curses.

The only one who recognizes me is the silent girl Durga. Not that she understands who I am, but she remembers me from that night in the temple. She has attached herself to Subbu, following him wordlessly, sitting where he tells her to sit. No other word has she ever spoken except Kanaka. Sometimes she still sings without warning, but more fantastic is the quality of her listening. For it has been noticed that sometimes when a song is sung or an instrument played, the hairs on her body stand on end and tears flow from her eyes. Young musicians who've heard that story travel here to sing in her presence, and famous musicians are careful to stay away from such an irrefutable test. Subbu recites his poems to her, keeping only those to which she responds, and in this manner, he is becoming a fine poet. Sometimes I sit nearby unnoticed and collect the pages he discards. A dancer could make much of such songs.

You have seen all parts of the temple. It is beautiful no doubt, but every temple in this land of temples is such as this. You could visit one a day for a year, and one more year, and a year after that, without exhausting the temples studded like stars in this countryside.

You came to hear the story of this temple's glory, and I've told you instead its secret, kept for these many years. You too have your secrets, and maybe one day you will tell me. Or not. You're safe, that's all I wanted to be sure. I understand your silence. Someone dying of thirst doesn't say, 'Teach me about thirst.'

If you think Kanaka devi will grant the desire that consumes you, pray to her. But what really do any of us desire? That someone who is sick gets well, that someone without a child gets a child, that someone who writes an exam passes, that someone who's turned away from us turns back. But things can only happen as they must. The illness that courses through a body must do its work, the child must be conceived in the usual way, the questions on the exam paper must be answered correctly. No god can exercise much control over those matters. Only love stops and starts again on a god's whim.

You may think, looking back on events, that there were different actions you could have taken, said yes instead of no, been cautious instead of daring, spoken at some moments when you did not speak, said nothing at some other moments when you did, held back instead of giving so freely. I can only tell you that it doesn't matter. All we can hope for is that sometimes our actions produce the results we intend. But what worked yesterday might not work tomorrow. Still, there is nothing more sacred than the labour of being. We are nothing but the turned earth of a ploughed field. And where the plough-point has gone, now the needle will easily follow.

Afterword

There is no clear line between fiction and non-fiction, one is always bleeding into the other. Consider this incident. More than ten years ago, I had a dinner party at my flat in Chennai. One of the guests told us what a devadasi had told him – that one of the girls in her lineage had turned herself into a gold statue in order to escape becoming the courtesan of a man she knew to be her father.

That I had a dinner party, where and when it took place, that a guest told this story, is fact. There is also good reason to believe that a devadasi told my guest the story he repeated, because he is a truthful person and knew many devadasis. But that a young girl turned herself into a gold statue, that couldn't be true. Or could it? The figure of Kanaka entered almost fully formed into my imagination at that moment. It was the desire to somehow make her story true that created the fiction of this novel.

V.A.K. Ranga Rao, the man who told the story at the party, became my most important source through many hours of interviews. He was born and brought up in a royal family, and devadasis were part of his life – Bangalore Nagaratnamma, a famous devadasi of the time, foretold his future involvement in the arts while he was still in his mother's womb. He knew several devadasis, who liked and trusted him enough to share intimate details of their lives, and he was generous, frank and perceptive in imparting his knowledge and experiences to me. While not implicating him at all in my errors or shortcomings, I couldn't have written the novel without his help and encouragement.

The anecdotes and incidents in the lives of particular devadasis told to me by Ranga Rao have been placed in the context of 1920s south India to accord with the available historical evidence. This was the time when social reformers were working to end what had till then been acceptable cultural practices, such as bigamy, child marriage, the maltreatment of widows and caste-based abuses. The practice of marrying young girls of a particular community to the deity of a temple in order to signal their sexual availability to wealthy high-caste men also came into question at this time. The age at which girls could be so dedicated was first raised to twelve, and then sixteen. Finally, Muthulakshmi Reddi, whose mother had been a devadasi, proposed a bill to end the dedication of young girls altogether in the Madras Legislative Assembly in 1927. It took another twenty years to become law because of the complexity of the devadasi's role, in which ritual work in the temple, an artistic discipline and concubinage were so intertwined.

The term 'devadasi' is applied to women from vastly different communities and time frames. As part of my research, I went to Gokak, in North Karnataka, to interview present-day devadasis. Though they don't share an artistic practice with Tamil Nadu devadasis, there are commonalities: they undergo a ritual in a temple, their 'first night' is sold and they are sexually available to upper-caste men. They find the designation a double-edged sword – it grants them a degree of freedom and at the same time comes with stigma and sexual obligations that they can't easily escape. In their conversations with me, these women talked about their sexual experiences with remarkable honesty, resilience and sense of humour.

I also relied on the bharata natyam repertoire. This dance form, which had once lived only in the bodies of devadasis, had lived in mine since I began studying bharata natyam in 1970. While working on abhinaya with Kalanidhi Narayan in the 1980s, I began closely reading the padams and javalis of poets like Kshetrayya, who wrote for and about devadasis. When writing the novel, I returned to this body of literature as a historical source of insight into the sensibility of devadasis – their emotions, their relationships and their daily lives from girlhood into old age at the most private and visceral level.

I lived for six weeks in an agraharam, or Brahmin quarter, near Tanjore, talking to other informants who had known devadasis, priests or zamindars and viewing source material at the Tanjore District Collector's Office and the Saraswathi Mahal Library. I conducted further research at the Adyar Theosophical Society Library and the British Library.

These periods of research were made possible by the generous support of the Ontario Arts Council, the Canada Council for the Arts and the Toronto Arts Council. The Singapore Creative Writing Residency, co-organized by The Arts House and the University Scholars Program, National University of Singapore, gave me the time and freedom to complete a first draft, for which I am very grateful.

Author image © Ashok Charles

A Note on the Author

Gitanjali Kolanad has been involved in the practice, performance and teaching of bharata natyam for more than forty years. Her writing is a continuation of her fascination with dance and dancing bodies. *Girl Made of Gold* is her first novel.

CRAFTED FOR MOBILE READING

Thought you would never read a book on mobile? Let us prove you wrong.

AN EXTENSIVE LIBRARY

Including fresh, new, original Juggernaut books from the likes of Sunny Leone, Praveen Swami, Husain Haqqani, Umera Ahmed, Rujuta Diwekar and lots more. Plus, books from partner publishers and loads of free classics. Whichever genre you like, there's a book waiting for you.

juggernaut.in

Ask authors questions

Get all your answers from the horse's mouth. Juggernaut authors actually reply to every question they can.

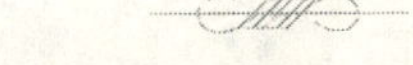

Rate and review

Let everyone know of your favourite reads or critique the finer points of a book – you will be heard in a community of like-minded readers.

Gift books to friends

For a book-lover, there's no nicer gift than a book personally picked. You can even do it anonymously if you like.

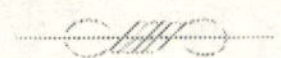

Enjoy new book formats

Discover serials released in parts over time, picture books including comics, and story-bundles at discounted rates. And coming soon, audiobooks.

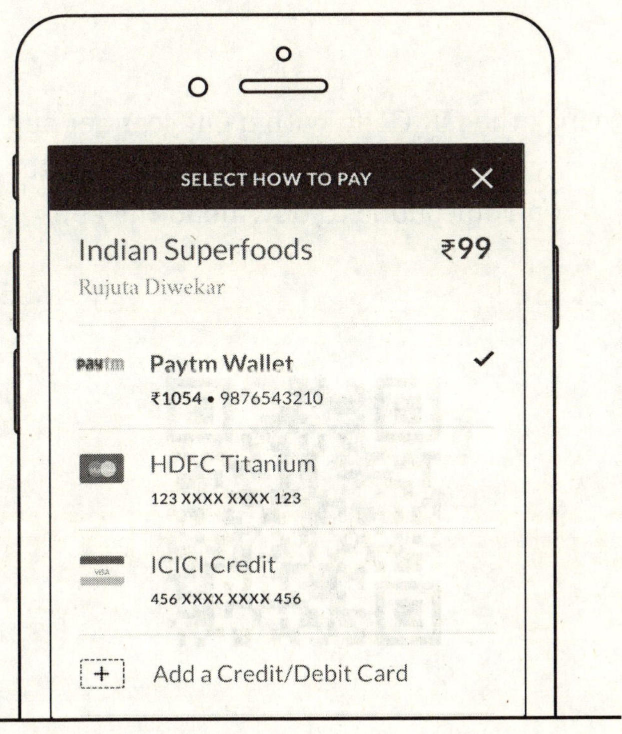

Paytm Wallet, Cards & Apple Payments

On Android, just add a Paytm Wallet once and buy any book with one tap. On iOS, pay with one tap with your iTunes-linked debit/credit card.

Click the QR Code with a QR scanner app
or type the link into the Internet browser
on your phone to download the app.